Songs in the Mountain:

Hartstown, Virginia, holds stunning natural beauty and a close-knit mountain community. Deep in the heart of Appalachian coal country, Hartstown also suffers more than its fair share of tragedy.

Beth Azen discovers a strange ability that leads her deep into the ancient mysteries of the mountains around her. Mark Hersch finds more than he ever imagined on his lifelong quest to heal the damage left by decades of mining.

Together, they discover the deadly nature of true loneliness.

A gripping tale of sorrow and redemption.

Legacy of the Land:

Elenda Murphy needs change like she needs oxygen.

Constant motion.

Extreme adventure.

Anything but standing still.

Her heart always as restless as her mind.

Then a shattered leg sends Elenda back to the bedrock of family.

An enchanting tale of destiny and free will.

In the Pines:

A ghost train carries a murderous secret deep through the North Georgia mountains. Betrayal colder than the wind blowing through the pines.

A young girl with a burden a hundred years out of time.

An old man's tale of guilt and regret.

A heartbroken woman caught in a mystery only she can solve.

A boy long past living holds the key.

Can unearthed secrets end the nightmare at last?

Fantastic Women: A Dark Fantasy Novella Trio

Copyright © 2018 by Kari A. Kilgore

All rights reserved

Published 2018 by Spiral Publishing, Ltd. www.spiralpublishing.net

Book and cover design copyright © 2018 by Spiral Publishing, Ltd.

Cover art copyright © 2018 by Elena Bulgakova/Depositphotos.com and Littleny/Dreamstime.com

ISBN-13: 978-1-948890-05-2

Library of Congress Control Number: 2018907791

Additional copyright information for previously published material at the back of the book.

For Virginia and Victoria Kilgore

*Fantastic women who opened a thousand doors
for everyone who came after.*

FANTASTIC WOMEN

A DARK FANTASY NOVELLA TRIO

KARI KILGORE

SPIRAL PUBLISHING, LTD.

CONTENTS

A gripping tale of sorrow and redemption.
SONGS IN THE MOUNTAIN
KARI KILGORE
AUTHOR OF UNTIL DEATH AND THE DREAM THIEF

For Jason
The best traveling companion I ever could have hoped for.

Chapter 1

Beth Azen leaned back in the squeaky office chair, rubbing her burning eyes. The desk itself wasn't much more than a countertop wedged in between overcrowded shelves and rows of filing cabinets. The town hall's scanner was old enough to give off a sharp, hot plastic smell after a couple of hours.

She'd worked in more than one musty archives room over twenty years as a writer, but this one in her native Hartstown, Virginia, had to be the most compact. Access to over a century of Boun County's history was worth a bit of discomfort.

Worse than her sinus rebellion against the aromatic space, Beth's fingertips were raw from handing dozens of glass plate negatives. The plates were a bit larger than a paperback and about a quarter of an inch thick, but heavier than they looked. The greenish edges were straight but wavy, like they'd been melted out instead of cut. Even through the sweaty blue gloves, she felt like she'd been rubbing sandpaper all day long.

Her nerves were just as frazzled. Beth wasn't sure if it would be worse to break one of the negatives, break the glass of the scanner trying to place one of them, or cut herself with who knows what had been on the razor-sharp edges for over a hundred years.

Most of the negatives didn't look like much, with one side

smooth and the other rough with varying shades of black and gray. The images Beth extracted from the persnickety things were gorgeous, though, more sharp and clear than almost any other medium. Photographers willing to lug chunks of glass though the mountains back then had her full respect.

Beth wondered if the to-be-scanned pile would ever be smaller than the finished stack in the box beside her on the gray carpeted floor. She always got to this point in a long project, when she felt like she was never going to get to the end. Knowing she'd get over that helpless feeling eventually didn't make any difference. Beth took a sip of cold coffee, at least two cups past too much, and got back to work, taking out another of the delicate slides.

The town manager didn't want anyone to bring in music or even use earbuds like most places did, but Beth didn't mind. She constantly had a song in her head, from the time she woke up until she fell asleep, and probably all night long, too. She'd heard it described as some kind of brain disorder on the radio a while back, but that didn't make sense to her. She couldn't imagine how bored people got if they didn't have something to listen to.

She lined the rectangular piece of glass up against the side of the scanner, put a blank sheet of paper over it, and lowered a huge square light to a couple of inches above everything. The lamp was bigger than what her dentist used, and the heat added to the closed in feeling in the tiny room. Nothing else she'd tried would bring out the old images.

Putting together a massive book of images with the town historical society wasn't one of Beth's typical non-fiction writing projects, but she enjoyed her side trips into book design and publishing. Her parents and her hound mutt Janie certainly appreciated her staying home for a few months instead of traveling for research. And she enjoyed the chance to wear her most comfortable faded jeans, old flannel shirts, and sneakers without asking about anybody's dress code. She flipped through the other photos on her screen while the scanner whined and clicked.

This corner in the Virginia coalfields struggled even now, but the poverty a hundred years ago was horrifying. The rudimentary houses and muddy roads didn't bother Beth nearly as much as the faces of the men, women, and children.

So many of them seemed much older than they could have been, understandable with a hard way of life and dangerous work logging or coal mining. The kids in particular looked as old as the photographs. Seeing that era coming to an end didn't disturb Beth at all.

A chirpy Minnesota-nice voice from right behind her did.

"Hey Beth! How's it goin' today?"

"Doing fine, Tina. You?"

"Great! Just checkin' to see if you need anything."

Tina had moved with her husband a year ago when he started teaching at the new optometry school in town, and she clearly loved everything about the change of pace from northern city life. Beth appreciated the interest, especially compared to being isolated in a cold, dank basement like she'd been on past jobs, but sometimes Tina was a little too eager to help. And today her strong, flowery perfume was one too many aromas in the tiny space.

"I'm good, thank you," Beth said.

"Just let me know, then."

Tina grinned and spun on her heel, her long blonde hair and pink gauze skirt throwing up a bit more of that thick aroma. Beth tasted the scent on the back of her throat, even over the strong coffee, and her head was swimming. She rubbed her temples, trying to fend off a headache. When the scanner clicked again and stopped, Beth froze.

Chapter 2

Silence. Not only the lack of grinding mechanical noise, but complete silence. For the first time since she'd been old enough to notice, her own mind was eerily quiet. Beth shook her head. She heard her short brown hair shifting, the low voices of other people in the conference room behind her, the tick of the cooling scanner, but nothing else. She even heard her own heart beating faster with every second.

Beth pulled off the gloves and grabbed her jacket, then darted out the side door before Tina or anyone else could stop her. She had to get some fresh air, even if it was well below freezing. She'd been working too long, as usual. Being stuck in a closet-sized room full of dusty and moldy boxes was getting to her.

She leaned against the red brick building, staring past the fire hall next door at the gray mountains dotted with dark green pine trees soaring all around the town. The only sounds in this sheltered alley were a few cars passing on the street and tree limbs creaking in the bitterly cold wind. Her hearing was fine, even sharper than normal.

In fact, Beth heard a low hum now, like an amplifier turned up too loud. That had almost drowned out the music before, but only when she was too tired or getting sick. Maybe it was time to knock off for the day. One of the best parts of freelancing in her hometown for a change was being able to go home at three if she needed to.

As she got closer to the archives room back inside, meaning to put everything away, shut down, and get out of there, Beth slowed. She turned her head from side to side, trying to figure out where the sound was coming from. A woman's voice, low and sorrowful, getting louder with every step she took. That didn't make sense with the strict policy about radios or music players, but Beth heard it all the same.

She glanced around the empty meeting room. All the office doors were closed and the metal folding chairs were stacked up against the walls. Beth shook her head and stepped into the archives room.

The voice split into many, all singing a dirge Beth had never heard before. She didn't recognize the language either. Some sort of European, maybe, hard to place. She pulled her phone out of her pocket, but it was set to silent. The computer didn't have speakers, and she didn't see any kind of intercom.

The singing shifted to an old-time funeral, clear even without hearing the words.

"That's enough for you today," Beth said under her breath. She picked up the last negative she'd scanned without bothering with the gloves, not worried about fingerprints for the moment.

Beth almost dropped the piece of glass when the singing got much louder. She carefully put it back down, and the noise level decreased. Beth raised the huge scanning lamp and held the image under it. A group of people sat and stood on a small hillside, all staring solemnly at the unseen camera. Long gowns for women and dark suits for men, hair in braids or buns, and elaborate hats, all from around the turn of the last century. Exactly like all the other photos she'd seen over the past few weeks. The freshly filled grave in the middle explained why everyone wore their Sunday best.

The singing died down for a few seconds, then they launched into one Beth did recognize. "Rock of Ages," but the words were oddly accented, hard to pick out. She caught herself trying to figure out where the singers had come from. The nationality of the mourners was the least of Beth's problems.

She packed up and shut down, relieved when putting the slide in the box on the floor muffled the singing. Beth would have felt a lot better if it had stopped altogether. She tapped her fingernails on the metal doorframe, contemplating asking Tina if she heard anything. Trying to imagine the response whichever way it went put an end to that idea. Beth closed the door and walked away slowly, the song getting fainter with every step. Even when she got in her car and turned on her own music, the strange voices never did disappear.

Chapter 3

Two days later, Beth was feeling more rough and sharp around the edges, just like those chunks of greenish glass, than she wanted to admit. The singing had only gotten louder, and now she heard people talking low and soft in between the songs. The sensation that she'd be able to make out the words if she only tried a little bit harder felt like grit inside her brain.

Walking into the archives room at the town hall made it worse. Handling the slides was almost deafening, but at least the music changed depending on what she was looking at. Sprightly, joyful fiddles, funeral dirges and hymns, schoolhouse learning chants, and even a bit of early bluegrass. Beth could change the tunes with different slides almost like a radio.

None of the other archived materials, whether postcards, printed photos, or newer plastic negatives, had an effect. Only the pieces of glass. The constant undercurrent was as maddening as her own music had been comforting.

Rather than go across the street for lunch, Beth got a fresh notebook and closed the door. No matter how stuffy it got, the last thing she needed was Tina or anyone else wandering in while she was talking to herself. She pulled out the funeral picture, the one that started all this strangeness. Murmuring voices replaced the singing, but she couldn't quite make out any words. A few more songs went by with no more success.

"Can you hear me?" she whispered, her cheeks turning red. She tried again, a bit louder. "Hello? I hear you talking. Is anyone there?"

The song continued without even a pause. Beth scrubbed her fingers through her hair, then got as close to shouting as she dared in the closed space with people right outside the door.

"Either tell me what you want or leave me alone!"

The voices stopped.

Beth tried to hold perfectly still, not sure if she wanted an answer or for the whole thing to be over. She could probably adjust to not having music anymore, but not to the constant noise.

The low, empty circuit hum in her ears intensified, and a voice floated up like a distant station on her great-uncle's old tube radio.

"Been wonderin' if anyone was thar." The woman spoke with a thick dialect that was hard to understand, but Beth thought it had to be from close by. "Been tryin' to get through for a powerful long time."

Beth opened her mouth twice before any words made it out.

"Trying to get through from where?"

"Well, from right here," the woman said. It sounded like rii-chyer. "Bountyfield. Ain't that where you are?"

"This is Hartstown, but I'm in Boun County," Beth said, leaning over to grab the computer mouse. She followed a hunch and scrolled through the manuscript file to the section about county origins. "This used to be called Bountyfield a long time ago, so I guess that's where I am."

"Well then, you aready know what I want."

Beth let out a short laugh, shaking her head. The list of what she knew sat pretty much at zero.

"No, ma'am. I'm afraid I don't know anything. Maybe we can start with why on earth I can hear you at all?"

"That question only you can answer. I been called a wise woman, a seer, sometimes even a witch, among my people. You anything like that?"

Beth shook herself and sat forward, scribbling as much as she remembered about the conversation so far. If nothing else, she wanted a record of such a vivid break from reality. Assuming she recovered, this would make a great story someday.

"I don't think anyone's ever called me wise," she said, smiling. "Not even close."

"It don't have to be you, now. If you hear me at all, some of your folks had an ear for such."

Beth tapped the pen on the nearly full page, trying to imagine what this mystery woman meant. Her concerns about having some kind of breakdown led her to the answer.

"I had, well, not exactly a wise woman," she said. "One of my great-grandmothers was supposed to have a little trouble with reality. I don't remember her very well."

Beth stopped, chills running down her arms and legs. Granny Johnson hadn't just had trouble. She'd heard voices. Voices no one else could hear. When the woman spoke again, Beth jumped hard enough to leave a mark on the page.

"Reality depends a lot on who's seein' it and who's callin' it, you ask me. What's your name? If we're gonna talk like this and get anything done, I need to know who I'm talkin' with."

"I'm Beth. Beth Azen. I guess I should have asked sooner, but what's your name? And what do you mean, get anything done?"

"I'm Clina Jane. What I mean is fix this pizen down deep in our mountains. I reckon more than enough lives been lost to it, certainly from where you're sittin'."

Chapter 4

Beth knew what Clina meant by pizen, but she hadn't heard it for a long, long time. She thought that dialect had just about died out around the time her family's reunions stopped. Her mind seemed to focus on the strangest of details today. A disembodied voice was telling her about poison in the mountains, and she was worried about the pronunciation?

"I'm glad to meet you, Clina, but I don't understand any of this. What poison? You mean the water?"

"Same as before, you got to tell me. Could be in water by now, sure. Do a lot of folks still die right around there, Beth? More than you can count for?"

For the first time since she'd heard the strange singing in her head, Beth wasn't confused. Digging into this book project showed her all too clearly how many mine disasters were in the county's past, with quite a few killed in timber and railroad operations as well. It did seem far too many for such a small town.

"Well, yeah, I suppose they do." Beth's mind kept searching through her internal files, more crowded but better organized than the tiny room she was in. A lot of people died in automotive accidents close by, too. And she knew of more drownings than made sense with the small number of creeks and one river. "I hadn't really thought about it, but Hartstown seems to be unlucky in a lot of ways."

"Unlucky may have been the trouble way back at the start, but things have gone a ways past luck by now. A bad wrong's been lodged down under the ground here, one that has to be made right. I been tryin' to get through to someone on your side for so long I like to give up. Now that I found you, Beth, we got to get busy."

"Hang on, I'm not even sure this is real," Beth said. "Any of this. Even if I had any reason to believe you, why would I believe some poison was down in the mountains causing trouble?"

"Look around and answer that second part for yourself," Clina said, her voice sharp and testy. "Might be able to help with the first part, though. Why'd you hear me in the first place?"

"Why… How the hell should I know?"

"Good girl, good girl." Beth was sure she heard chuckling in her mind, raspy and satisfied. "Got some backbone after all. Jes tell me what you was doing when it started."

"I was scanning these old slides," Beth said, wishing she had something to scowl at. "Old photographs, pictures."

"Now you're on to it. Like as not I'm in one of those pitchurs."

"Well, it's a whole group of people. We couldn't find any names for this one."

"That don't matter. Listen to me, now. We never did pitchurs less it was something big like a wedding or a funeral, maybe a baptizin'. What kind you got there?"

"A funeral," Beth said, her heart pounding. "For a coal miner."

"Makes sense. That's who we mostly had em for, and way too many a those. Can you tell the name on the stone?"

Beth picked up the slide in shaking hands, making sure she had a firm grip on the sharp edges. This was one of the batch the historical society had rescued from someone's basement. The years of damp hadn't done the glass any favors.

"I'm sorry, that part's too dirty and smudged."

"Then why don't you clean it?" Clina sounded like she was talking to a small child. "What's the point of having a thing if you leave it too dirty to use?"

Beth snorted, feeling like her mother was lecturing her about keeping her room clean. The reason she'd accepted a few weeks ago when starting research for the book sounded pitifully thin to her ears. Some part of her knew Clina wouldn't be happy with her explanation.

"For these I'm not supposed to. We have to leave the slides as they are so they won't get damaged any further."

"I never heered of such nonsense. If you're wantin' some kind of proof, you just have to get you some soap and break that little rule right now."

Beth sat back in her chair, shaking her head. She didn't want to lose access to the archives, but not doing simple cleaning had been driving her crazy. Probably not as crazy as never figuring out what was going on inside her own head would.

"Okay, Clina. I can't use soap on these," Beth said, laughing at the surreal argument. "Hang on, I've got some water right here."

She picked up her water bottle and pulled out one of the tissues she always carried in such a dusty environment. Turning the slide over first to make sure she had the smooth side, not the coated side that held the photo, Beth tilted the bottle into the tissue for a second. She rubbed the slide in a circle big enough to include the tombstone, trying to make the edges uneven enough to look natural.

"I see…looks like Fekete."

Clina was silent long enough that Beth started to wonder if the whole strange episode was over. Maybe she'd backed the delusion into a corner asking for proof she could only provide with her own eyes. She was glad she'd put the slide down when the voice spoke.

"That'd be Gez Fekete, died in 1908. I know the very pitchur you have there. Look to the left side of his stone, where the trees are, then count three people from the end. You're lookin' at Clina Jane wearin' my finest."

Beth leaned closer, then turned to the computer. She found the image in a few seconds and zoomed in on the mourners more than her eyes ever could have. The women and children stood together in a group behind dark-suited men. The third one in was a slender woman wearing a long white dress with a dark belt, standing with one hand on her hip. Beth saw pale skin and dark hair under a huge, white hat.

"I see you just fine, but that doesn't really prove anything," Beth said, feeling a little guilty, even if she was talking to herself. "I can see this for myself."

"Sounds to me like I did good when I got through to you, Beth. You might have enough smarts to get this thang done. Tell you what, go look in whatever records you got there under Gez Fekete. He was from way off over the ocean, Hungary, I think. Even printed his last name before his first like they did over there. He married a girl from Bountyfield, and his five kids was born here. The last 'un just a few weeks before he met his end under the ground. You'll find his missus changed their name over to Black once he was gone."

"Records," Beth said to herself, closing her eyes. "They have census records next door at the courthouse, marriage records too. Anything else you think I'll find while we're at this?"

"Now I don't mind one little bit that you don't believe me. That's why you're the right one for a tough job like this. Go on and look up a thang or two on me, then."

Beth leaned forward and wrote the dates, names, and places Clina gave her. She didn't know whether verifying everything would make her feel better or worse.

"I'll go check this out." Beth put all the equipment on standby and picked up her bag and jacket. "I'm assuming I'll still be able to hear you over there, so you'll know how it's going."

"You have right many questions only you can answer. Seems to me you can hear me best when you're with those pitchurs, but I reckon we'll find out."

Chapter 5

Beth walked back into the archives room two hours later, nose running terribly from the midewy records room at the courthouse. The floodwaters from a hundred years ago might never have receded by the way the huge old record books destroyed her sinuses. Under her discomfort, she was dazed and more than a little afraid.

"Clina? I'm back. Can you hear me better?"

"Clear as a bell, Beth. Find that proof you was lookin' for?"

Beth sat down hard in the creaky old chair, not sure how to answer. She picked up the glass image of the long ago funeral scene, her fingertip touching Clina's white hat. Might as well start talking.

"Everything you said checked out, down to the dates when they had them. I don't understand how or why, but you're telling me the truth. How do you remember things so clearly?"

"It's the only way I know to remember. I kindly think I'm still back here, when all this is going on. At least some part of me is. Reckon we can work together and clear out that pizen I told you about?"

Beth laughed louder than she meant to, but it felt too good to stop. At least until she started sneezing out the mildew. Five in a row took care of most of it, not very neatly.

"And exactly how do you propose we do that?" she said, trying to catch her breath. "I still don't know what poison you're talking about."

"Now that you decided to believe in me, maybe you'll believe in this. Thar's a tiny little mine pit, operated before I was born, and all the big ones around it claimed many a life. More than their fair share, some say. The trouble all goes right back to one of the first men to go under the ground after coal for his house. First one to die, too."

"What happened to him?"

"Rock fall far as I know, same as killed more than's ever been counted. The way it happened ain't the problem. Fact is this man was so far off away from home when he passed. His bones rest there still, deep in that pit where he died."

Beth rubbed her arms, trying to soothe the hairs standing on end. Her grandfather had spoken of going down in the mine and never knowing if even his bones would make the trip back up. No one knew for certain how many met that fate long before anyone kept good records.

"That happened a lot, certainly with all the disasters here," she said. "How could one man make the land poison?"

"That one man came from across the water, too, a place where the dead was buried together back to the beginning of time. Great, long graves, where even poor folk was kept from being alone after they drew their last."

"How can you possibly know this, Clina?"

Beth didn't want to say it, but she couldn't imagine the education of a woman born in these mountains so long ago went far enough to cover burial mounds in Britain and Europe.

"I hear him is how. He's been singing, crying his lonesome heart out for all this time. Folks still livin' and breathin' catch his song in their bones, on the backs of their necks, in the goose walkin' over their graves. Once you pass on like I have, you hear his cry so loud and clear you can't ignore it no more."

"What's he crying for?" Beth whispered.

"I reckon what he wants is company. And he's done all he can to make that happen. I know a touch from when my husband died years before I did. A body so lonesome pulls others to him any way he can. Out of the rock, out of the air, out of the water. That's the pizen that's filled this land full of so much blood and sorrow."

Beth jumped so hard she grunted when someone knocked on the metal door. Damn, she'd forgotten to close it when she came back in. She knew her face was bright red before she turned around, but there was no help for it.

"Hi Beth, how's it goin'?"

"I'm just fine, Tina. You startled me is all."

"I'm sorry!" Tina said, putting a ring-laden hand over her heart. "I just wanted to remind you we're closin' a little early for the community forum. You can stay as long as you like, but it's gonna be noisy. Big crowd tonight."

Something tickled at the back of Beth's mind. An alert from her investigator's instinct that she knew better than to ignore, but she couldn't catch it.

"Great, thanks for the warning."

When Tina walked away, Beth finally heard people gathering in the conference room. Chatter and movement were loud in the normally quiet space.

"Sorry, Clina. I think we might be done for the night," she said, keeping her voice low. "I can't sit in here and talk to myself with the whole town outside the door. Half of them thought I was crazy for going away to college and again every time I leave to work on a story. The other half think I'm crazy for coming back."

"Sounds to me like you hit it just about right. You in a hurry to get home to your own man?"

"Not at the moment," Beth said. She didn't want to respond the same way she did when some of her relatives asked about her single status over and over again. "Just me and my dog."

"Dog's company, but you should have you someone to talk to in the middle of the night. That's some powerful lonely time."

"You're right." Beth started to put the slide back in the protective box, then paused. "Listen, I'm still not sure what you think I can do for this miner. I don't even know where to start. How could I possibly find him?"

"I might could point you in the right direction, then I reckon it's up to you," Clina said. "You'd likely find him easier than you think. This thing in your head that lets you hear me might not be so easy to turn off. It might well work for him and a bunch more folks besides."

"Perfect. That's just what I need," Beth said as she shut everything down. "A bunch of grouchy oldtimers carrying on inside my mind all the time."

"Might find you learn a thang or two," Clina said, and Beth was sure she heard laughter. "No way to know til we get there."

Chapter 6

BETH CLOSED the door behind her before she got a look at the room. Almost all the metal chairs facing her were filled, and a thousand people seemed to be staring. Clammy sweat covered her body in an instant. She tried to smile, then walked as fast as she could toward the exit.

Just as she reached the door, she glanced back over her shoulder. The stack of brochures on the long table beside her set her inner alarm off again. The state department of land reclamation's information about…old abandoned mines.

Beth didn't much believe in coincidences, especially not this big. She turned around and took a seat near the back. Clina and what sounded like a hundred of her friends were singing hymns again, soft and low in her head.

Over an hour later, Beth stood in the corner while it seemed like everyone else in town lined up to ask questions. The presenter did his best not to look at his watch, but he clearly had somewhere else to be. Beth willed him to wait just a few more minutes. When the last person finally headed out, she walked up to the front.

"Listen, I'm sorry to bother you," she said, holding out her hand. "I won't take long. I'm Beth Azen. I know you need to get out of here, but I might be able to help you get the word out about this project."

"Good to meet you, Beth," he said. His grip was warm and firm. "Mark Hersh. Any ideas you have would be great, but I'm afraid they want to close up here."

"Well, no, we can wait a while longer," Tina said from a few feet behind Beth. She was smiling, but she glanced at her husband and two little boys out in the hall. The kids were as blond, blue-eyed, and pale as their parents, but they spoke as if they'd lived in Hartstown all their lives. "Beth would be a great contact for ya, Mr. Hersh. She's a reporter and a writer."

"Maybe we should talk then," Mark said, his bright green eyes lighting up with his smile. He was just over Beth's height of five-eleven, and he seemed to be in his mid-thirties too. "It's so hard to get through to small landowners when we only have rumors about where some of these old mines were located."

"Oh, she's just perfect, then!" Tina said, beaming. "Beth's been here for a few weeks workin' on a history book about Boun County."

"That's what gave me the idea," Beth said. She hoped the strange turn her project had taken didn't show on her face. "If you haven't had dinner yet, we can walk over to Rayburn's."

"Sure, I'd like to hear more," he said, then turned to Tina. "Thank you again for the room, ma'am."

As Tina locked up behind them, the boys ran screaming into the once again empty space. Beth was still a bit in shock over basically asking a man out to dinner, one she'd never laid eyes on before tonight. At least he was easy on the eyes.

"Just as well we got out of there before those kids exploded," she said as they walked across the street in the harsh wind, only having to wait for a couple of cars at just after seven. "When did you start focusing on these smaller mines?"

"We're still working on several big ones, but a lot of the stream runoff in Boun County seems to be coming from these old, unpermitted mines. No one really kept records for a long time. Once they did, a bunch of the smaller ones were already abandoned. Cleaning up these little mines has been a pet project of mine for a while. Finally starting to happen."

Beth's mind worked at top speed as they got settled in the Italian-themed restaurant. Murals of Roman statues and ancient city vistas contrasted with the red vinyl booths and college basketball game muted on two flat-screen TVs hanging from the ceiling. The food here was hardly gourmet, but it was good. Her stomach growled at the rich, yeasty smell of pizza and frying potatoes.

She tried to think of all the reasons he'd turn her crazy idea down. If Beth managed this, she might solve more than Clina's problems.

Chapter 7

"So what's your idea to help out?" Mark said, pulling off his blue state jacket and running his hands through his unruly strawberry blond hair. He was dressed as casually as she was once he shed the official uniform, with blue jeans and a faded burgundy Virginia Tech t-shirt. "And tell me more about your book."

"Those two kind of go together," Beth said, taking a drink of her Coke to buy a bit more time. This had to be good. "A couple of days ago, I was scanning a pitch…a picture of a coal miner's funeral from the turn of the last century. I remembered reading about how they sometimes didn't have anything to bury, especially with a rock fall or a bad explosion. I'm sorry to be morbid, but do you come across anything like that when you're re-mining?"

"Now there's a different sort of question," he said, blinking. "As a matter of fact, we've come across bones that are clearly human a few times, especially in these pre-regulation mines. Strange as it sounds, that's part of what got me into this line of work. When I was fifteen, I found a leg bone in an abandoned house coal pit I never should have been inside of. Were you thinking of writing about that?"

"Kind of. What do you do with those remains?"

"So far we've just been storing them unless we can identify anyone who was killed in that specific mine. A bunch of them are unclaimed." He sat forward, his expression more curious than confused.

"Well, something else I'm writing about for this book is the cemetery in town," Beth said. "It's not far from right here. It's pretty amazing, really. The markers are in almost a dozen different languages. Most people don't realize how many immigrants came here to work in the mines back then. There's also a mass grave they used after a couple of the big disasters."

Beth watched Mark's eyes, hoping he would put the rest together for himself. Clina's singing inside her head kept her calm instead of putting her on edge for the first time. If she could get this to work out, and if Clina's hunch about Beth being able to hear more than one voice was true, the mystery miner might have his community resting place after all. Mark rubbed his neatly trimmed reddish beard, then nodded.

"You know, that's not a bad idea," he said slowly. "I have family in the town cemetery, but I didn't know about the mass grave. If we put the bones there and you write about it, we could create some sympathy and good publicity for our program and for your book."

"We could, but I was thinking we could do something sooner to get people involved with what you're doing." Beth sat back as the waiter delivered a gorgeous pepperoni pizza. She wanted to dig in, partly to quiet her constantly rumbling stomach. Partly to put this off, even if she did scorch her mouth. "How about if we go into one of the mines that's rumored to have bodies inside, see if we find one, and write about it?"

"You are optimistic!" Mark said with a grin, sliding two steaming slices onto her plate before doing the same for himself. "That would be great, but you have better connections than I do if you can find a long-lost miner on the first few tries."

Beth laughed, trying not to let it get away from her. If he only knew…

"I've been through a lot of records lately," she said. "And I'm a pretty good investigator. I've tracked down things far less likely than this. Think we could give it a try?"

Mark took a bite and hissed cool air over his tongue. He shrugged.

"I'd have to pull some serious strings to get you in on one of these jobs. We want to take care of these runoff spots, but the other thing is these old mines are dangerous. Rotten timber, no roof support, definitely no ventilation fans."

"How about this, then," Beth said, encouraged that he hadn't said no. "I'll pull my research together and ask around a little. If I find a likely spot, I'd bet the possibility of finding someone will get you access to the land. Then if you do find something, go ahead and shore things up. Make it safer. Right before you're ready to seal the mine, I go in, take pictures, and we get the bones. I promise you that story will get you access to a whole lot more land."

Beth took a bite of her cooler and absolutely delicious pizza, the crispy crust, soft cheese, and sharp pepperoni seeming like the best thing she'd ever tasted right then. Either Mark would like the idea, or he wouldn't. There were plenty of obstacles, assuming she could even hear another voice besides Clina's, not to mention the safety issues. But if he wasn't interested, she was stopped cold before she even got started.

"That may just be too good to pass up," he said, nodding and staring into space. "We don't go in expecting to get coal out of most of these individual mines, so no worries about antsy operators hoping to get their investment back breathing down my neck. Mainly get in there, check it over, get anything dangerous like old black powder or dynamite out, and seal them up."

Mark looked into her eyes, and Beth was surprised by warmth in her belly that had nothing to do with the pizza. She'd been so caught up in trying to work the story angle that she hadn't realized just how cute he was. And his ring finger was bare.

She would have sworn she heard Clina chuckle deep inside her mind.

Chapter 8

"So, are we on to something here?" she said, and immediately blushed at how her words and thoughts matched up. He saved her by picking up his transparent plastic soda cup.

"Well, we're probably into a mess of regulations and red tape, to tell you the truth, but I think it's worth a try. To our future grave robbing adventures!"

"May they all rest in peace." Beth tapped his cup with hers.

She wished they had beer or wine instead of fountain soda, though too much booze would send her mind off in even more inappropriate directions. This bizarre situation Clina had dragged her into might turn out to have pretty damned good side benefits.

"I suppose we should get to know each other better if we're getting into such a macabre business together," Mark said, seeming to echo her thoughts. "Did you grow up in Hartstown? You don't quite sound like it."

"I grew up here, but my mother grew up in Chicago. I think her accent tempered dad's a bit, and we visited up there a lot. If we're talking accents, you don't sound like you're from here at all."

"That's where I'm sneaky," he said, raising one eyebrow with a crooked smile. "My parents are both natives. I was born here, but I grew up all over. Dad was in the Air Force until I was twenty. When he had long vacation time, we always came right back to Boun County."

"Odds are good we crossed paths some summer or another," Beth said, liking the sound of this more and more. Too many men she dated in college or on jobs refused to consider moving to such a small town. "Did the state station you here because of your family?"

"Wouldn't that be nice?" he said, shaking his head. Beth hoped her face didn't show how fast her heart sank. "We haven't had a full-time person down here for a couple of years. I've been reminding them I'd be perfect for the job for a few months. I'm only here for one more presentation, over in Abrams in the morning. Then it's back to Richmond."

"Oh," Beth said. She managed to keep from sighing. "I guess I misunderstood. I thought you… I thought these projects were starting up right away."

"Don't worry, I'll be back in a couple of weeks," Mark said, then it was his turn to blush. The ruddy color in his cheeks just made him look like he'd been hiking or running or something equally athletic. "Wow, did that sound overly confident. I meant we'll have preliminary funding in place by then. If I can give them a list of agreeable landowners, that might even speed things up."

"In the spirit of being overly confident, I'll do whatever I can to help." Beth hoped her recurrent blush was as attractive as his was.

By the time they shared a serving of banana pudding, agreeing it wasn't as good as their grandmothers made, Beth was more determined for herself than for Clina or the mysterious miner. Mark was the most interesting person she'd met in a long time, and by far the most interesting guy. Even if she had to convince a dozen cranky landowners to let them search for forgotten mines, every outcome she thought of was good.

"Looks like we're closing another place down," Mark said as he intercepted the check. "This was obviously a business dinner, so the Commonwealth should pay, right?"

"Obviously. You staying with family in town?"

"Yeah, for this trip," he said, rolling his eyes. "If I get something more permanent, that won't work out for long."

"I lasted about two weeks with my parents when I got back from college." They laughed together, and she turned to let Mark help with her coat. He put both hands on her shoulders for a second, more than long enough to get her full attention. He was smiling that gorgeous smile when she faced him. Beth gave him the card she'd dug out while he was paying for dinner. "Talk again when you're back in town?"

"I hope we'll talk before that," he said, handing her a business card. "My personal mobile is on the back."

"Then I'll speak to you soon."

Chapter 9

Beth gritted her teeth and slowed down for yet another gigantic rut in the overgrown gravel road. This narrow path through the thick brush and trees didn't have any kind of sign or number, only a faint blue trace on the thick book of county maps she'd checked out from the library. A few half-rotted trees, thankfully not quite blocking the way, made it clear no one else had been out here for a long while.

She'd also borrowed her brother's old four wheel drive work truck, knowing her sporty sedan wouldn't have a chance on these old farm and logging tracks. This was still a bigger challenge than she'd expected. Several well-maintained modern mining roads she'd already checked out were much easier to drive on, but they hadn't brought her any closer to that lonesome abandoned pit.

"Horse warns you of road trouble, not the other way round," Clina said.

"Yeah, I guess they do. This would take a month on a horse instead of a couple of days, too. Just let me know if you hear him getting closer."

After a good bit of contemplation about how quickly she'd lose access to the archives if something went wrong, Beth had carefully packed up the funeral slide for these trips to make sure she could at least hear Clina. She was nowhere near as confident as her ghostly guide that she'd be able to hear the lost miner, much less figure out where he was.

"Who you wantin' me to listen out for? The miner or your new feller?"

Beth laughed out loud, then slipped the transmission back into four low for what looked like exposed boulders in a washed out section of the roadbed. She'd gotten used to conversations with a disembodied voice faster than she ever would have imagined.

"I hear from Mark often enough. You listen out for the miner."

The truth was not more than a few hours had passed without at least a text message from Mark since their pizza dinner a week ago. Beth knew she wasn't alone in looking forward to their long, flirty conversations more and more. Mark had flat out told her so the night before. His return in another week felt impossibly distant to her.

"I was wondering how we should approach this," Beth said. "Even after we find the right pit. Maybe I should have a false start or two instead of going right there. That would look a lot less suspicious."

"Here I was thinking you had smarts enough for this job. You forget this poor lost man has killed more folk than anyone's been able to count up? Like you told me, he ain't exactly limited himself to miners."

"I know, Clina. I just think it will seem too strange if I lead Mark right to a body on the first try."

"You mean if it seems like you did your research job, like you said you would?"

Beth rubbed her cheek in front of her left ear, trying to get the annoying ringing to stop. Bobby's truck rattling was so much noisier than her car.

"I only said I was thinking about it," she said. "We have a little more time."

"We have time as long as this 'un don't try to pull more souls under the ground with him," Clina said, her voice sharp. "That'd be a ways past too late."

"I hear you, I hear—"
"Hush now! You're hearing the wrong thang!"

Chapter 10

BETH PULLED over to the side of the narrow mud and gravel road, happy to avoid another giant rut right through the middle. She leaned forward and rubbed her face again, then gasped. That wasn't ringing in her ears. The tone was shifting, modulating from flat noise into a rising and falling song. Tears filled her eyes at the mournful sound even though she couldn't make out any words.

"Is that him?" Beth whispered, looking around.

She spotted a huge, modern coal storage tipple just over the ridgeline to the right, the squared-off, pale blue tower sharp against the bare trees and dark gray winter sky.

"That's who I been hearing all these long years. We're right near where all the troubles happen, ain't we?"

Beth pulled out her phone, amazed she got reception. Once she got a look at the real-time map, she understood why. This felt like a long-forgotten road in the middle of nowhere, but the middle of Hartstown was over the ridge to her left. If the old pit was close by here, it was no wonder things happened all over town as well as in the mines. Several of the giant ruts she'd driven across led to a good-sized creek on the other side of the road.

"We're close by the Mossy Rock #5 and #7 mines," Beth said, zooming the view out on the map. "Several disasters right here over the years, yeah. And town is just over the ridge. The cemetery is on the other side of this same mountain."

"No wonder I hear him so clear. Can you find out who owns these parts nowadays?

"I don't have to find out," Beth said, smiling despite the sorrowful cry echoing through her head. "This side belongs to Art Steffens, an attorney in town. He's in the habit of buying up land that's been mined or logged and planting hardwood trees. I can't imagine he'd object to cleaning up a dangerous old pit, especially on the state's tab."

"Well then, get your squeeze on that phone thang and get to work!"

Beth shook her head, driving forward and listening to the wailing getting louder. After about a quarter of a mile, the voice got weaker. She backed up until it was at an agonizing peak, so loud she could almost understand the words. She marked the spot on her map and on the phone, wondering if she'd be able to tolerate getting much closer. Her throat and chest felt like they were filling up with heavy, warm water, and more than a few tears spilled over.

"I still don't know about that, Clina. Hey, there's a gully, a gap in the trees, too. Might be a trail from a long time ago. I'd bet that's where we'll find our pit."

Beth heard a sigh, almost as loud as the singing.

"Wish you wouldn't waste my time and yours, tryin' to make a good impression on that feller. Seems to me he's impressed enough with you. If he's half as great as you tell me, I can't figure what either one of you's waiting for."

"Well, being in the same town instead of five hours apart would be an improvement," Beth said, trying to make mental notes of everything around her. "I've got three landowners on board already, so it won't take long. I'll go talk to Mr. Steffens right now."

Chapter 11

A few hours later, Beth grinned when she saw the number on her phone. The icy rain was too heavy to go outside, so she settled for closing the archives room door before she answered.

"Hey there, Mark."

"Hey Beth! I saw your email just now, fantastic! How'd you get so many people on board so fast?"

"I warned you," she said. "It's my irresistible charms. They let me dig into things no one else could because I make sure they enjoy every minute."

"I understand exactly how they feel," Mark said in a low voice. Beth smiled and closed her eyes, glad no one was there to see her. More than her face was warmer than usual. "Seriously, though, getting Art Steffens on board is huge. He probably owns several of those old pits, and the streams on his land feed right into the river. Well done."

"Thank you, sir," Beth said, wishing she could thank him in person. "So do you think this will help speed up your funding and starting work?"

"Well, that's why I'm calling, to warn you. When I told the project manager how much land we'll have access to, he said we need to get started before everyone changes their minds. How's tomorrow sound?"

Beth laughed, hoping she'd covered the handset in time. She didn't want Mark or anyone else to know just how good that sounded, at least not until she was ready.

"I do appreciate the warning," she said, "but I'm afraid I can't get out of town fast enough to avoid you. What time do you get here?"

"Should be late afternoon if I can get enough things wrapped up here. Then we'll get started the next day. Did that killer investigator's mind of yours give you a hint of where we should dig in?"

Beth's smile faded, and she was glad Clina was busy singing work songs with what sounded like a herd of school kids. Maybe it was some kind of nagging guilt about insider information or something equally silly, but she was still worried about hitting the jackpot on their first try.

"I was thinking the Fleming place out near George's Gap would be a good place to start. I'd be more than happy to help you with directions and introductions, Mr. Hersh."

"That's something else I need to talk to you about, but I believe I'll keep it to myself until I see you in person."

"I'll look forward to your visit even more, then," Beth said. She flinched at an ear-splitting siren, one that had to be coming from the fire hall next door. An alarm had never gone off while she was so close. "Mark, I'm sorry, I have to go. Sounds like we have a fire or something here."

"Yeah, I hear that. Hope it's nothing bad. I'll give you a call tonight."

Chapter 12

Beth opened the door to general chaos, more than she'd ever seen in the town hall. Every office door was open, and several grim-faced people ran through in different directions. Tina was standing just inside the exit door, talking into her cell phone and crying. When she turned and saw Beth walking toward her, Tina met her in a tight hug.

"What's going on?" Beth said.

"There's been…" Tina stepped back, wiping at her face but barely able to talk. "A school bus went off the road heading out of town. Right into the river."

"Oh no," Beth whispered, her hand on her chest. "Are your boys okay?"

"No one knows yet. That's why they took the fire truck, in case the ambulances aren't enough. They won't let me go with them, even though I'm right here!"

Beth put her arm around Tina and looked at the fire hall's open door, and Beth knew they were thinking the same thing. A town this small didn't have a whole lot of rescue equipment or people trained to use it to begin with, certainly not for a bunch of kids caught in a nearly frozen river.

"Can I get you anything, Tina? I'm so sorry, but I don't know what to do."

"No one can do anything until we know more," Tina said, then seemed to pull herself together a little. "Listen, they're going to bring the kids who aren't hurt here to get warmed up and meet their parents. School was already out and we're closer. They need to keep the hospital clear for…the worst ones. It might get crazy."

"I'll wait and see if I can help," Beth said, wishing she could leave and avoid all of it. "Let me know, okay?"

Tina nodded just as her phone rang. Beth went back into the archives room, sick at her stomach. She didn't want to know the truth, but not knowing would drive her crazy. The voices in her head were singing old mountain dirges, further twisting her guts.

"Clina, I need to ask you something," Beth said, pulling the door around but not closing it. "Did we upset the miner? Being out there this morning?"

The singing stopped, but no one said anything.

"Come on, I need to know. Something awful just happened here. I can't send Mark or anyone else out to that pit unless—"

"I don't rightly know what makes him do what he does," Clina said in the softest voice Beth had heard from her. "His wailin' got louder after we was out there."

"I can't let Mark go walking in there," Beth whispered. "Once this miner gets a living person in that pit, he could bring the whole mountain down."

"I know you're afeared. I am myself. But if we don't do something now we got the chance to, he'll keep on forever. I got blood on my hands cause I only now got through to someone after decades trying. I done the best I could. Can you tolerate being among the living, the ones that's sufferin', and lettin' it go on?"

Beth sat forward with her elbows on the table, heels of her hands pressed against her eyes as if that could keep the tears inside. She could still smell Tina's flowery perfume on her clothes, still feel the panicky tightness of her hug. No one yet knew how bad this latest disaster was, but Beth was certain she knew what caused it.

Clina was right about not being able to live with letting it go on.

But she didn't know if she could live with letting Mark be some kind of sacrifice, either.

"Is it even safe to bring his bones out of the mountain?" Beth said, shivering. "We have no idea how many people he's killed. Won't he get worse if he's not under tons of rock?"

"I'll not lie to you, Beth. You're the first to ever hear and try to help, and you deserve the truth even if it pains me to tell it. I don't rightly know if he'll get worse. All I know is how bad he's been up to now, and that he's cryin' out from bein' so lonesome. I can just hope he'll calm if he's here where I am and lots of others too."

"Can you help me, Clina? If I can manage to at least get close when Mark goes in there?"

"I swear to do everything in my power for you, and all the souls here with me swear the same."

Beth heard more voices, gathering up and getting louder, wordless affirmations that echoed and blended into one long hum.

Mmmm-hmmm. Mmmm-hmmm.

Chills covered her body, rising and falling with that internal reassurance. She had one last deep, strong fear about her own sanity, about trusting her life, Mark's and anyone else involved to ghosts, real or imagined.

"Well, everything you've told me checks out so far," Beth said, sitting back and wiping her face. "I don't have a lot of choice except to keep going."

She heard the first whimpers and cries of children coming into the conference room behind her. Beth went out to help, dreading how bad it would be and hoping she could finally bring these long nightmares to an end.

Chapter 13

BETH PACED in her living room, bare feet cold on the hardwood floor. She was too distracted and upset to do anything about that. Janie was curled up on the couch, her long red ears and black eyebrows shifting every time Beth passed by. Her heaviest hiking boots with thick socks tucked inside waited beside the front door. She planned to need those not long after Mark arrived.

Getting started tomorrow was no longer an option.

She glanced out for at least the hundredth time, wanting to see his state agency sedan turning up her driveway. Her brother's old truck was still out there. Beth hoped the abandoned road to the old pit wasn't impassable after the downpour of the last twenty-four hours.

She'd been a coward the night before and all day today when it came to telling Mark what was going on, sending him text messages instead of talking. Beth couldn't find the words, and she knew everyone in the state and the whole country would have heard by now.

Five out of the twenty-three children on that bus had drowned or given in to the awful cold after being caught in the water. Most of the rest were injured. It would have been a terrible tragedy anywhere in the country, but it was a disaster in this small town. With barely one hundred in the whole school, everyone knew who those lost kids were. Beth knew all of their families herself.

One of Tina's boys had a broken arm, the other a broken leg to go with many scrapes and bruises. She and her husband were like all the others who took their children home last night or could visit them at the hospital today. Relieved it hadn't been worse for their own family and struggling with sorrow and guilt for those not so lucky.

Beth's heart pounded when Janie barked at the sound of a car outside. She turned in time to see Mark getting out. A tiny part of her that wasn't heartbroken or terrified thought he was even more handsome than she remembered, his hair glinting in the sun coming through the last of the rain clouds. He waved, but he didn't smile. Beth went out to meet him.

"Beth, I'm so sorry about all this." She made it into his arms before she started crying. "Are you okay?"

"No, not really. I'm glad you're here."

He stroked her hair, and all Beth wanted to do was stay right there. Just go back inside, build a big fire in the woodstove, have dinner, and go to bed. Not to make love, though she'd been daydreaming about that more than a little until yesterday.

Now she wanted nothing more than to curl up safe and warm and go to sleep. She took a deep breath, then drew back to look into his eyes. Try as she might, she couldn't come up with a clever or calm way to explain anything, and she was out of time.

"Come on inside," she said. "I have some strange things to talk to you about."

After a few minutes of inspection and mutual approval between Mark and Janie, he and Beth sat facing each other on the couch. Despite the droopy eyed hound head on his knee, the confused look on Mark's face didn't make starting this conversation any easier. Clina whispered inside Beth's head.

"You got everything you need to take care of this terrible thang. We'll be with you, and if he's half the man you think he is, he'll do all he can."

"I can't think of any other way to say it," Beth said. "I want to go out to one of those pits. Now, this afternoon."

"Hang on, we don't have everybody here yet," he said, his brow wrinkling.

"That's why we need to go now. I know they're not going to want me go in there, but I have to. I promise you I'll explain everything someday."

"Well, that was the thing I hadn't told you, Beth. My boss thinks we'll get the whole project off to a bigger start if we do your story as soon as we can, and he wants as much publicity as we can get. If we can get Mrs. Fleming to agree and everyone signs waivers, you can go inside with us right from the start. I'll have a photographer here tomorrow."

Beth smiled, surprised at how good a simple change in her facial muscles felt after the last several hours. If all the strangeness and sadness disappeared, she'd be delighted to have such an exciting story coming together. Almost as delightful as Mark's fingers twining through hers. His warmth lightened the sorrow of funeral songs she'd been hearing all day long in her head.

"That's great, thank you for setting that up," she said, squeezing his hand. "This is something a little different. I'll bring my camera. I can just about guarantee you we'll find the first set of remains tonight."

"What's going on? Have you heard something new?"

"You could say that. Did you bring enough gear for both of us?"

"Wait, I don't understand," Mark said. "The crew's on board with you going inside. Why does it have to be tonight?"

Chapter 14

BETH LOOKED OUT THE WINDOW, picking out the tipple they needed to go toward on the other side of town, the pale blue now vivid against the slate gray mountains, trying to find words that wouldn't make her sound crazier than she felt. She remembered one of the first things Clina said to her.

"This is going to sound strange." Beth looked into Mark's eyes, hoping the nervousness churning in her belly didn't show on her face. "Did you ever hear talk about a wise woman or a seer when you were visiting here? Anything like that?"

"My granddad had dreams no one could explain," Mark said without hesitation. "He always knew when something bad was coming, especially people dying. I don't think any of my family would have mentioned it anywhere else we lived, but every single one of us knew to heed his warnings. Never knew him to be wrong, either. He told me it came from his own grandfather, but I've heard of the same with women. Are you telling me you're a seer, Beth?"

Her heart and her breathing seemed to stop, but words found their way out anyway.

"Not exactly," she said. "At least I don't think so. I haven't seen anything, but I believe I'll be able to take you to a lost miner who needs to come up out of that mountain as soon as we can get to him.

I can… I hear him. I know right where the pit is, at least where to park and start hiking."

Mark didn't frown, let go of her hand, or even raise his eyebrows.

"You believe this miner has something to do with what happened here yesterday?"

"I do," Beth said, trying to keep her trembling chin and voice from running away with the rest of her. "That and a lot of the other bad luck that lives and breathes in Hartstown."

He stared into her eyes for a few terribly long moments, then nodded.

"Fair enough. I brought respirators and gear for both of us, out in the car. Some axes and shovels, too, but the big equipment won't be here until tomorrow. Think we can get Mrs. Fleming's waivers handled first? Her son called me this morning. Sounded like he's going to want to argue for a while before he'll get out of the way and let her sign."

"You're right about her son, but that's the best part," Beth said, letting out a breath she didn't remember holding. "This mine is on Art Steffen's land. His office is right across from the town hall, and he's been asking me nonstop when we can get started."

Mark smiled, and Beth's eyes filled with tears. These weren't the hot, painful tears she'd shed too many of since yesterday and most of the night, the ones she'd been trying to fight back all day. These were tears of relief from the deepest part of her.

"I've got the paperwork with me, too," Mark said. "We'll take care of that on the way."

Chapter 15

Beth parked the truck and rotated her shoulders, trying to work out the tense knots from the trip. She'd had serious doubts more than once. The creek was much higher than before, and the ruts all had deep standing water. Her first trip out gave her a good idea which parts to aim for, but not one part of the drive had been easy.

"Good driving, Beth," Mark said. "I never would have made it. Too much city living. Here, let me."

She turned toward the driver's side window, and he dug his strong fingers into the worst spots. Good as it felt, Beth was staring through a long crack in the glass directly at the gap in the bigger oak and maple trees. Between that and the wailing, she'd never be able to relax. The lost miner was far louder than he'd been just a couple of days ago.

"That's a huge help, thank you," she said, facing Mark. "Listen, we're going to have to be careful here. This guy's been trying to pull people down there with him for a long time."

He looked out the window past her, then focused on Beth. She was afraid she'd gone too far, said one too many crazy things.

"We'll do our best. Mr. Steffens knows where we are, and I sent a text message to a couple of the crew on the way. I didn't tell them much, just that I got here early so we're going to check it out. If we can get to him, what are we supposed to do?"

"Remember the mass grave I told you about?" Beth said. "I hope if we put him in there he'll rest easier."

"Makes sense to me," he said. "Let's see what we can do."

Before she could talk herself out of it, Beth put both hands behind his neck and pulled him into a kiss. In that heat and touch, she forgot everything. Her sadness, her fears, her uncertainty that they should be out there at all. Beth held on to the one thing she did know. Her lips and Mark's were meant to be together.

"Now I'm about a thousand times more determined to get back out of there," Mark said, his cheeks flushed and his breathing faster. "Hear anything that might help us?"

Beth took the chance to catch her own breath as she grabbed her backpack from behind the seat. She pulled out Clina's glass negative and unwrapped it.

"Whatever it is seems to be linked to her," she said, touching Clina's white hat. "She's the one I'm hearing. I thought I was crazy at first, but I checked out a bunch of things she told me over at the courthouse. Every word was true."

Mark took the slide by the plastic-covered edges and held it up to the sun, still up but moving lower.

"How old is this? Do you know who—"

He touched the image and nearly dropped the glass, catching it against his thighs. He turned to Beth, tears in his eyes.

"The crying voice. Is that what you hear?"

Beth's jaw dropped, and she heard Clina and a few other people laugh.

"That's who we're here for," she said. "Do you hear anyone else? A woman?"

"No," Mark said slowly, holding the slide up again. "Just a man. I don't think I could stand to hear anyone else. Do you hear others?"

"I do," Beth said. "She's the main one, and she promised to help us as much as she can. I'll do my best to explain it all once we're out of here."

Mark leaned forward and kissed Beth again, humming deep in his throat. He put the slide carefully on the seat between them.

"We better go before I lose my nerve," he said. "Or before it gets too much later. It won't matter while we're inside, but I can't imagine the drive out will be easier in the dark. Sounds to me like we're heading up that little gap there."

"The road gets a little clearer from here," she said, "but the sooner the better. I can't tell you how glad I am you hear him, too."

"You and me both." Mark winked and opened his door. "I like you too much to think you were losing it just yet."

"Okay, Clina," Beth said under her breath when he closed the door. "We're here. We could use all the help you can send us."

"I got a big crowd gathered up waitin' for you. Some here think they knew the man in life. One even knew your feller, there, when he was a tiny boy. We'll do every little thang we can. Might manage some big thangs, too."

Chapter 16

THEY BOTH WORE OLD JEANS, heavy boots, and thick flannel shirts. Even with temperatures in the mid-forties, they'd be plenty warm hiking up the mountain. Mark was waiting beside the truck with knee and elbow pads, a bright yellow helmet with a light on the front, clear plastic goggles, and a dark blue respirator. Instead of the full face device she'd feared, it was only big enough to fit over her nose and mouth. There were three round fan-like openings at the bottom, and he held it by two straps.

"This one isn't heavy duty enough for hours in an active mine," he said. "But it should be fine for what we need. The full crew will have bigger gear with air tanks and all."

"I'd rather not have anything bigger than this," Beth said. "I don't think I could breathe in one of the whole face ones."

They slipped everything into her pack, and Mark handed her a short black metal shovel. He clipped an old but well cared for machete to his belt and grabbed a pickaxe, pointed on one end and flat on the other.

"You'll do just fine," he said. "It took me a while, but I finally got used to it. Ready to see if we can help this poor guy?"

Beth's nerves, on edge since she'd first seen Tina crying the day before, threatened to close her throat. Neither of them had any idea what they were walking into.

"Mark, he's killed a lot of people over the years. He probably had something to do with what happened yesterday."

"Sounds like more than enough reason to see what we can do to get him out of here," he said, taking her hand. "I don't think I've heard a more lonesome sound in my whole life. I know company makes me feel a whole lot better."

After about ten minutes of hiking up the muddy gully with several stops to clear the tangled undergrowth, Beth stopped. The narrow path ended ahead of them with a stand of huge oaks and poplar trees easily a hundred years old. They stood on a small level patch with higher ground close by on both sides, but there was another gap to the right. Only a few scrubby trees and low brush grew there, and Beth was sure she saw a darker area behind them.

"Do you hear it stronger over there?" she said, pointing.

Mark turned his head that way and nodded.

"Much stronger. Looks like an opening, too. I've never seen this on any map of old mines. Could be a house coal pit. If we looked around a bit more, I imagine we'd find what's left of his homestead."

Once they cut and pulled the brush away and moved a fallen tree limb, they found a gap between the rocks almost as tall as Beth. They could easily pass through one at a time. Scattered black bits of coal stood out along the dark gray rock underfoot. The singing was nearly a scream in her mind.

"Is this it, Clina?" Beth said under her breath.

"You found the very place. We're gonna do what we can, but you best be careful there, you and your feller."

She watched Mark wipe sweat from his face, then swing his pack to the ground. He smiled at her, that ruddy flush in his cheeks again, looking more excited than afraid.

"We will."

After helping her with the gear and making sure the respirator was fitted properly, Mark settled it down around her neck.

"We'll see what it's like in there," he said. "These house mines usually aren't all that deep. If we stir up too much dust, we'll be ready. Let me know if you hear anything strange, all right?"

"Yeah, you too," Beth said. "Clina thinks it was a rock fall, so we need to keep an eye on the roof."

They turned on their lights and headed into the cave. The floor was fairly smooth, with gouges in the rock that looked like they were cleared long ago. Coal or dust had settled on every surface. After the fresh, humid air outside, Beth wrinkled her nose at the dry, musty smell. She was starting to worry about smelling a man dead for at least a hundred years until she saw piles of leaves and sticks on the floor. Something small had nested here a long time ago.

"You don't think this is big enough for a bear to be sleeping in, do you?" Mark said, stopping in front of her.

"The stink would be a lot stronger than this. Black bears smell like garbage dumps. I think that's the least of our worries."

After about ten feet, they saw the start of the coal seam on the left wall. It was narrow at first, just a few inches around Beth's shoulder height, then dug out when it got a little thicker further on. The gouged out shelf got thicker and higher until it blended into the gray rock above them.

Beth felt like all the bones in her body were vibrating with the keening that seemed to be all around them. She couldn't quite catch the words the group in her head was singing, but the tune sounded a lot like "Barbara Allen." She couldn't imagine how such tragic lyrics could help. Mark stopped again, pulling a much brighter flashlight off his belt.

"We've got to be close judging by his cry alone," he said, his voice not much more than a whisper.

He moved the light slowly along the roof, stopping when the fairly smooth black and grey expanse gave way to a huge jagged hole. As he lowered the beam toward the floor, it turned from clean white to dingy gray. The dust and dirt came from above.

"Get your mask on, Beth."

Chapter 17

MARK PULLED his mask up with his free hand, then took a step backward. Beth moved with him. Before she could say a word, several large pieces of coal and rock fell, the noise deafening in the tiny cave. A chunk of limestone easily two feet wide and three feet long landed where he'd just been standing.

"Safe bet he knows we're here," Beth said, her voice muffled by the respirator. "You okay?"

"I'm good. I think we found our man."

She followed the light and saw pale white through the shifting dust. The skull and arms were unmistakable, as were the long leg bones. The torso was hidden by a pile of rocks, none of them as big as the one that had just missed Mark.

They'd obviously been big enough.

The man's arms and fingers had been stretched out toward the entrance for decades, desperate to escape his hellish trap. Only his voice and malevolent spirit had ever made it.

"Clina?" Beth said, her stomach roiling at the thought of anyone trapped in a black hole like this.

"You done made it to the right spot." Voices still sang in the background, but Beth heard Clina loud and clear. The miner's mournful singing had turned to screaming. "He's not happy 'bout you bein' there."

"Can you help us?" Beth said. "We can't get him out if he's going to drop rocks on our heads."

Mark turned to watch her, eyebrows raised, but he didn't say a word.

"Grab on to your feller so maybe he can hear me." Beth took Mark's gritty hand, and they both jumped when Clina shouted. "Now listen here! These folks mean to help you! I don't plan to spend another hunnerd years tryin' to get you away from there. Stop actin' a fool and let them take you out!"

"Clina?" Mark whispered. Beth nodded. "Is it safe now?"

"I have no earthly idea," she said. "He still sounds angry to me."

"He's right full of piss," Clina said. "We got him pushed back a mite. I feel like if we hold tight to him, kindly surround him, he might understand."

"I don't feel reassured," Beth said. "Can we do anything to help?"

"Besides carryin' him outta there? Try doing the same. Think on holdin' him wrapped up like in a quilt. I make no promise, but I hope that helps him to feel safe."

"Did you hear that, Mark?"

"Try to wrap him up in a mental quilt, and no promises," he said, and Beth saw the smile in his eyes above the mask. "I was thinking more of putting him in a backpack, but I'm glad to do whatever works."

They stepped forward over the huge rock, Mark's flashlight still aimed at the roof. The dust was starting to settle, but both left the respirators on. When they got close enough, Beth saw more of what happened. The man's spine was damaged. Two of the vertebrae in the middle of his ribs were compressed in a strange way.

"I'm sorry I don't know your name, sir," Mark said, focusing his attention and the light on the bones. "We're here to bring you out and give you a good burial. Will you let us do that?"

"You heed that feller now," Clina said. Beth had let go of Mark's hand, and he gave no sign of hearing. "These good people aim to help you."

Mark shrugged his pack off and knelt beside the skull, still glancing uneasily at the roof. The voices with Clina rose as the miner's got quieter. A huge crowd singing "Amazing Grace," Clina speaking the words right before the group answered, was louder than his low moan.

"We do want to help you," Beth said, joining Mark on the rubble strewn floor. "We can take you to a place where you won't be so lonesome."

Beth heard the whispery fracture just as Mark reached toward the skull, a split second before Clina and everyone with her shouted in her mind.

"Mark!"

Chapter 18

Beth launched herself sideways onto her hip, shoving Mark away, wincing when his helmet smacked against the wall. Before she could move, more rock dropped from the roof. A thick chunk of coal landed on her upper arm, knocking her flat. The pain was immediate and huge. Beth screamed, the miner's voice shrieking an answer.

"What happened?" Mark shook his head, his words slow. He sat up and found her with his headlight. "Beth!"

"I think it's just my arm," she said, her voice tight.

She gritted her teeth when he helped her sit up. She'd have bruises from the rest of the rocks, but Beth was sure the bone was broken.

"That's it, we have to get out of here," Mark said. "Can you stand?"

"No, wait," Beth said. "This is why we came in here. I can't let this go on."

Beth looked at the bones when she spoke, doing everything she could to direct the words toward the lost miner. Her arm was throbbing every time she breathed, but she couldn't just walk away.

"It doesn't matter why. Not anymore." Mark picked up his pack and the flashlight before he reached for her good arm. "This roof is unstable. We can try again with the full crew."

"No!" Beth shouted. Mark drew back, and she fought down her urge to apologize. That wouldn't get her anywhere right now, and it could get both of them and who knew who else killed. "Clina, I need you all to help me now. We have to make him understand."

The voices in her head stopped, leaving her inner ears ringing in the silence. The miner's voice whispered like the wind on a bitter night.

"Mark, help me," Beth said. "I need to stand up so we can face him together."

He held her with one arm around her waist and the other supporting her good hand, but Beth cried out more than once before she was on her feet. She gripped Mark's hand and looked at the skull now covered with dirt.

"Listen to me," Beth said. Clina and many others repeated her words in a dozen accents. "I know you're alone and afraid. We're the first people in a hundred years who can help you. We can take you out of here right now. If you try to hurt us again, we'll leave you here. We'll come back tomorrow and blow this place up. You'll be alone for all eternity."

She paused, and Clina spoke into the silence, the echoes a few seconds behind.

"Not a one of us'll speak to you no more. We done all we can to tend to you, but you tried to hurt my friends. The wall of cold and empty I will build up around you will make your deep hell seem like a fairy land o' milk and honey."

The air around them seemed to compress, the dust frozen in place. Another huge pile of rocks tumbled down from the roof a few feet away. Mark drew Beth back with him.

"Beth, please, we have to get out of here."

"There are a hundred people underground, in the mine just across the creek. Some of them haven't buried their kids yet. Not even the roads are safe anymore. We have to get him out of here."

Beth stepped forward into the shifting dust.

"We have a place ready for you. You'll be with a bunch of other people. Clina and her friends will make sure you're safe. Please don't make us leave you here alone now that we finally found you."

"I know you hear me right now," Clina said, her voice gentle. "Let them take you out of there, and we'll make sure you're never lonesome again."

The whispery voice in Beth's head grew louder until she realized the air in the cave was actually moving. She took a step back despite her determination.

"It's moving out," Mark said, squeezing her hand. "The air's clearing out."

He swung the flashlight around, and the beam shone cleaner by the second. Before Beth could count to ten, not even normal cave dust was visible. She let go of Mark's hand and lowered her respirator.

"I think we got hold of him for now," Clina said. "Don't know how long we can keep him, so best get to movin'."

"Thank you," Beth said, to the miner, Clina, and Mark. This time her words were echoed in many languages. Italian, German, French, and several she didn't recognize. "We want to take your bones from this place and bury you with a great group. They'll welcome you home."

"We surely will," Clina said, and again voices from different parts of the world joined in.

"I'm a son of these mountains just like this woman is a daughter," Mark said. "I know the pain of being far off from home. Let us do what we can to calm your soul."

Chapter 19

MARK KNELT AGAIN, holding a trembling hand over the skull for a few seconds before he touched it. For the first time since Beth first heard it, the miner's voice fell silent. Mark gently picked up the skull and slipped it into his pack. Beth squatted as carefully as she could and picked up the left upper arm bone, then the right. Within a few minutes, they'd shifted the original rock fall aside and gathered up everything they could see.

"Thank you for letting us help you," Beth said, her voice trembling from worsening pain in her arm. Sweat cut tracks through the grime on her face. "We'll bring you out of here, and bury you as soon as we possibly can."

"I know just the place for the night," Mark said. "Right beside my grandfather. They might have a lot to talk about. Come on, we need to get you to the hospital."

He pulled off his flannel shirt and tied it into a makeshift sling. Her arm still hurt, but the relief was dramatic.

"Sounds great to me," she said, kissing his cheek. "As long as we get our friend here settled first."

"I have an idea of the answer, but is there any point arguing with you?"

"None at all."

The soft breeze continued as they walked back out of the cave, clearing the dust and dirt in front of them. As soon as they stepped outside, a rumble built from deep within the pit. Beth heard rock falling in a wave, moving toward them in slow motion. Mark pulled his respirator on again and helped Beth with hers just as a thick plume of dust burst outward.

Within a few seconds, the air was still. Any sense of movement, of life, inside the abandoned pit ceased to exist. The brush and trees on the outside were coated an eerie pale gray all around them. Mark held his light out far enough to light up the entrance. Neither of them could have fit back through the rocks piled up there.

Beth leaned against a huge oak, trying to slow her breathing. She appreciated the humid but much colder air more than she would have ever imagined. The orange light was fading all around them.

By the time they made it back to the truck, Beth leaning on the shovel or Mark's back for the worst parts, she was trembling with cold and agony. When he loaded everything into the bed of the truck except his own pack, she saw gooseflesh rippling his bare arms. She tried to reach her right pocket, but it hurt too much.

"Can you get the keys, Mark? The road's a lot better from here on out. I don't think I can manage driving."

"Of course. Come on, I'll help you up."

Once they were settled in the truck with the engine started, the pack on the floor between them, Beth remembered the negative on the seat.

"Mark," she whispered. "Look."

The glass was shattered into dozens of pieces, but none of them had moved. The image was still perfectly aligned and clear.

"Our miner's last victim," Mark said, his eyes wide. "Can you still hear Clina?"

"I hear them singing. 'Auld Lang Syne' of all things. It's kind of perfect."

"It is," he said, resting his hand on her knee. "I just realized we forgot to get any pictures."

Beth laughed hard enough to jar her arm, but she barely felt it. She covered his hand with hers.

"We'll do better next time. Assuming Clina will help us out again."

Mark leaned closer to the pieces of glass and picked up one of the larger ones. He held Clina's face and her big white hat in his fingers.

"I have a feeling she will."

Chapter 20

THE NEXT AFTERNOON, Mark and Beth returned to the town cemetery half an hour before the groundskeeper was supposed to meet them. She'd been on the phone most of the morning getting this impromptu burial arranged, wanting to be certain nothing would interfere with the heartbreaking funerals taking place over the next few days. Beth's right arm was in a thick cast from right below her shoulder to just past her bent elbow. At least the break was clean.

"Want to stay here and I'll get him?" Mark said, parking his blue sedan.

"I'll go with you."

She did let him manage the tricky business of opening the door.

The Hersh family plots were in the shaded, hilly part of the cemetery, some of the oldest ones still left. Three rows back from the road stood an average light gray stone set right into the hillside. Mark leaned around and picked up his backpack, undisturbed from the night before.

"Walton Mark Hersh," Beth said, her fingers tracing the engraved words. "Were you named after him?"

"Sure was," he said. "No matter what my sister or cousins say, I was his favorite. Can you still hear anything?"

Beth reached into her jacket pocket to touch the fragment of glass, the sharp edges wrapped with plastic. While they'd waited at the hospital, Mark had told her about an artist who could coat the edges in metal and seal the whole thing to protect it. She'd already decided to let him do just that. Copper would suit Clina perfectly.

"Still right here, not that you need the likes of me," Clina said, and Beth was sure she was smiling. "You done good, Beth, you and that man of yours. His granddaddy is right proud a both of you. Says that one you rescued chattered a blue streak at him all night long. Couldn't understand a word, but he was glad to listen. I reckon we'll puzzle it out."

The voices in the background sounded like some kind of party gathering, maybe an old church social. At least a couple of fiddles were tuning up.

"She's there," Beth said. "She says your grandfather is proud. And that we did good."

"We did." Mark smiled and put his arm around her waist, careful not to touch her cast. "I'm glad Papaw approves. Do we know much about our miner yet?"

Beth heard a deep voice, one she'd only heard crying or screaming before. She couldn't make out the language, but he sounded calm. And happy.

"Not yet," she said. "The senior Mr. Hersh said he was a bit hard to understand, but they're working on it."

"Good. Let's get him laid him to rest."

The state photographer and groundskeeper were waiting by the low black crypt marking the mass grave. In the end, the procedure was remarkably simple. The burly, bearded man worked the edge of a long piece of iron under the marble slab and shifted it several inches to the side. A metal chute led down into darkness.

Mark laid out white cotton flannel they'd found in Beth's sewing stash. The photographer clicked away while they lined up the bones on the fabric, then rolled it into a neat bundle.

"May your rest be easy," Mark said, holding the bundle over the chute.

"And your troubles be few," Beth said.

"We welcome you home with open arms," Clina said, and a chorus raised up with her.

The miner was singing again, but this time it was the sound of pure joy.

Mark let the fabric slide down into the grave. Beth stepped forward with a smaller bundle he'd helped her make that morning, slipping it after the bones of the lost miner. The glass made a barely audible jangle at the bottom.

"Thank you, Clina Jane," she said. "I hope to hear from you again."

"You best count on it, Beth. Likely be busy for a spell though. Gotta put your miner to work. We need all the help we can get makin' these little young'uns welcome."

An enchanting tale of destiny and free will.

Legacy of the Land

KARI KILGORE

Author of Songs in the Mountain and The Dream Thief

To my Granny, Clinas Kilgore

For her love of travel,
her love of reading,
and her love of family.

Chapter 1

THE CITY, the block, the whole neighborhood were exactly as Elenda Murphy remembered. Swarms of yellow taxis charged through crowded streets, horns honking to announce every penny added to the meter. Herds of pedestrians floated through an endless dance with the cars, interlaced flowing streams, crossing but rarely touching. Huge city buses lumbered through the chaos, moving eddies in the endless currents. The compulsive motion was so strong, so deep, that it echoed under the streets and in the skies above.

The building itself hadn't changed since before Elenda's parents were born less than a mile away. The light gray stone with red brick accents stood for years before the attack on Pearl Harbor thousands of miles away from New York City. More than half a century later, toxic debris and dust from the World Trade Center piled against the windows and seeped inside, even so far north in the Upper West Side.

Still the building endured.

Elenda's family intended to dwell here until humans were no more. She'd been the first in three generations to leave for college and never return. In more than ten years since she'd moved out and started her own life, not a thing had changed.

Nearly as constant was her mother. Marian Murphy's hair got

longer and shorter, with a brief, ill-advised flirtation with permanent waves captured in photos from decades gone by. The rich, dark red color never wavered, though. Marian proudly declared that she would not go gray as long as stylists needed the work. Or in a pinch, or some sort of apocalypse, as long as she could do the job herself.

Marian's wardrobe varied as subtly as her hair did, with only shifting hemlines, heel heights, and jewelry marking the years passing. The fine, wool suiting, either black or dark gray, pantsuits or dress suits with shoes to match, were as reliable as the ball dropping in Times Square.

Elenda knew her own wardrobe of t-shirts, blue jeans, and Birkenstocks distressed her always appropriate mother. Almost as much as the curly brown hair she sometimes didn't bother cutting for months at a time. The habits she'd picked up during her teen years to play up that distress had settled into an odd style of her own. She hardly could have survived her life as an extreme adventure vacation leader with a trunk full of high heels and silk blouses.

When she was being unusually honest with herself, Elenda admitted she was as predictable as Marian. Once she recognized that flash of herself in her stubborn mother, a fragile peace and friendship grew between them. Not nearly as easygoing as her bond with her easygoing father, but satisfying all the same.

Marian parked her car, the latest in a long line of dark blue Mercedes, under the huge burgundy awning. The doorman, the only doorman Elenda could remember, darted to Mrs. Murphy's driver side door. His uniform matched the awning, down to the gleaming brass fittings.

"Mrs. Murphy," Dwight said as he opened the door. "Welcome back."

"Don't fuss over me," Marian Murphy said, flipping her hand toward Elenda. "My baby girl needs the help today."

Elenda knew her face was bright red just as well as she knew asking her mother not to call her baby girl wouldn't do any good. She did need the help. Dwight drew back and nearly ran around to her side of the car. Her arms worked just fine, but he swept the door open so fast the car rocked.

"Surgery went well, then, ma'am?"

"Very well, thank you," Elenda said. With the massive cast turning her right leg into a dead weight, she took Dwight's offered arm to pull herself out of the car. "You know I can't stand being called ma'am. I have more than enough nicknames to choose from."

"Sure thing, Len," Dwight said. His grin let Elenda know he enjoyed the exchange as much as she did. "How long you here for?"

"She's here just as long as she needs to be," Elenda's mother said. "She's welcome to stay forever and a day if she wants." She stood behind Dwight, beckoning to the junior doorman. "Please bring my daughter's things up."

The young man hovering behind Dwight's shoulder was the first new thing Elenda had noticed since they'd left the hospital. Dwight pulled her crutches out of the back seat. Refusing to accept a wheelchair was one battle Elenda managed to win in this whole procedure. She settled the handles into her already bruised armpits and made her slow, hesitant way toward the revolving glass doors.

"This thing will be on for at least six weeks," Elenda said, finally answering part of Dwight's question. She wasn't ready to think about the *at least* part of that sentence. "Just depends on how long it takes my kneecap to heal."

"Then you have your physical therapy," Marian said, nodding once. "Use the side door, sweetheart. That will be so much easier."

Dwight was already halfway to the main doors to lock them open, something he routinely did for deliveries. He glanced at Elenda. She half-smiled and nodded. She couldn't afford to get into battles before they even made it inside. Not when her first real challenge, and the one she'd been dreading since these arrangements were made weeks ago, waited in the lobby.

Chapter 2

THE ELEGANT BRASS continued throughout the echoing, dark green marble floored room. The mellow gleam lined the front desk, mailboxes, and even the seams between the massive slabs of rock. The attention to detail reflected the taste and healthy budget of the building's designers, Elenda's distant ancestors.

The most elaborate, and most expensive, display was the antique elevator. A mere twenty-two steps had carried Elenda past the terrifying thing and into the staircase at the back of the lobby ever since she'd been old enough to throw a big enough tantrum to make it happen.

The elaborate bars and spirals of the elevator's double doors had long ago been covered with glass. Despite everyone telling her it was to protect the original fittings, Elenda was certain one too many little girl's fingers had fallen victim to the ancient elevator.

Her own had in countless nightmares as far back as she could remember. Her mother's tales of how much freedom and lack of supervision she'd had growing up in the 1970s only confirmed that certainty.

An arc of brass numbers and a matching arrow above the door warned of the impending arrival. Perhaps worst of all, at least on this floor and before she stepped into the claustrophobic box, was the key. Again under glass like some kind of sinister crown jewel, a long brass skeleton key hung beside a keyhole.

The fire fighter's access explanation rang hollow to Elenda at age eight and still at twenty-eight. The elevator car was shaped like nothing more than a metal cage. A fearful, and powerful, part of her mind insisted that key would never be enough to get the victim out of that cage once it slammed closed.

"Suppose you won't be taking the stairs on this visit," Dwight said, echoing her thoughts.

Elenda knew she'd never make it up eight flights even without the snail's pace as she tried to work out how to navigate on the slick floor on crutches. She'd either pass out from the pain of the cast dragging on her hip, or she'd miss a step and add a broken neck to her surgically rebuilt kneecap.

Still, she considered.

"She'll be just fine on this perfectly safe elevator," Marian said. Her flawlessly outlined red lips compressed before she smiled. "Your father made a point of checking on the most recent inspection, Elenda. Three weeks ago."

"That's wonderful timing," Elenda said. She flinched when the bell rang. Hopefully no one saw it. "Right around the time I had my little adventure on a perfectly safe staircase."

The doors were still for a second, long enough for hope to flare in Elenda's chest. Maybe the damned thing was broken. The left door slid behind the right one then, quickly enough for her to notice the burgundy carpeted floor of the car settling to almost level with the white marble threshold.

"A staircase?" Dwight said. He stepped in behind the young man with her bags and her mother, holding one hand in front of the door to keep it from closing.

Elenda gripped the crutches with sweaty palms, wondering if her pounding heart would be enough to send her crashing to the floor. The thought of being half in, half out, with those doors poised to take out her middle, got her moving.

"I was avoiding another creaky old thing like this one," she said, letting go of one crutch so she could hold the cool polished rail. "On a ski trip in Colorado. I did great on the slopes, but fell down the main staircase on a tour of the hotel."

"A ghost tour," Marian said, amusement plain in her voice. "Her girlfriends say one of the spirits pushed her."

"It was spirits all right," Elenda said. "One too many pumpkin whiskeys down at the bar."

The door slid closed, sealing Elenda inside with her mother and the two men.

She wanted to close her eyes as well, but that felt like courting trouble. The bars and spirals on the walls were also covered with glass, and glowing white plastic buttons took the place of hand operation. The handle was still there, though, perpetually locked into the neutral straight up position. The brass panel with raised instructions about emergency operation were somehow not the least bit reassuring.

"The same thing since she left for college," Marian said. She glanced at Dwight with on eyebrow raised. "My baby girl does all these absurdly risky things outdoors. Whitewater rafting, skydiving, mountain climbing. Never even a scratch. But get her indoors and all hell breaks loose."

"Bones too," Elenda said with a tight smile.

Her stomach rolled when they lurched into motion. She stared at the letters on the emergency panel, the paisley-patterned carpet, the glass and brass fixture in the ceiling. Anything to avoid looking at the diamond-shaped window in the door. Elenda had no desire to see what was floating past, or what waited on each of the floors as hidden steel cables lifted them upward.

"Well, you just let me know if there's anything I can do for you," Dwight said. His thick gray eyebrows were drawn down along with the corners of his mouth. Elenda knew he'd noticed how badly she was sweating.

"What she needs most is rest," her mother said. "And staying off her feet. Easier said than done with this one, ever since she took her first steps."

The door started to open before they stopped moving. Elenda's hand slipped on the rail, hot and slick now instead of clean and chilly. She hoped whoever got in here next wouldn't touch it.

When the floors were finally level, everyone stepped out, with Dwight once again holding his hand in front of the door. Marian Murphy turned right and disappeared, bustling down the hall. Elenda walked as steadily as she could out of the box of death.

When her foot and both crutches were on the solid, unmoving dark brown carpet, she remembered to breathe again. Elenda didn't care whether Dwight understood the reasons for her lightheadedness. She was grateful for his hand on her shoulder.

"I'll be fine from here, Dwight," she said, dropping all formalities now that her mother was out of sight. "I doubt I'll be leaving this apartment before it's time to get the cast off."

"Then I'll be praying for you, Elenda." He grinned as he walked with her down the hall, keeping pace with her hobbling progress. "On a more useful note, seriously, don't hesitate to let me know if you need anything at all. If I can't take care of it myself, I'll find someone who can."

Chapter 3

Elenda waited in the hall with her eyes closed, breathing deeply, willing everyone else to stay in their apartments. There were only three others on this floor, so if the proverbial luck of the Irish were with her indoors for a change, she'd be fine. Two of the three units being occupied by her own elderly relatives and her careful scheduling during her parents' workdays increased her odds considerably.

Six weeks to the day had passed since she'd ridden the elevator up here, just as she'd expected. She'd managed to survive forty-two long days and nights of intense interest and attention from not only her parents, but from each and every one of her family members living in the building and across the city. Several added to the fun by making the trip from out of town for her twenty-ninth birthday a couple of weeks ago.

A huge stack of library books, on-demand movies, and video chats with her friends got her through. A bit of the whiskey that helped lead to this, shipped by those friends from Colorado for her birthday, filled in the gaps once she didn't need the pain pills anymore.

She heard the whoosh before the chime, and felt the brush of air from gaps around the door. Only one door up here, but still that same brass under glass. Another key, out in the open unlike the one downstairs, gave the residents of the family penthouse floor the option to turn the elevator to express or access the basement and subbasement. A leftover from her great-great-great-great-grandfather's reign as builder-owner that struck Elenda as incredibly selfish with only one elevator in the building. That and she wasn't sure why anyone would want to get down below the foundation if they weren't forced to.

She stepped forward, steady with the crutches despite her unease with where she was. Weeks of practice and her insistence on moving under her own power made all the difference. Her stomach dropped when the elevator did.

Elenda met the waiting hospital shuttle van, more determined than ever to return without her massive plaster anchor. She knew physical therapy and building her strength back up awaited, but anything had to be better than the endless weeks she'd just been through. After more unlucky injuries than she cared to admit, she had the recovery steps down to a science. This would be a literal walk in the park.

She'd never been more mistaken in her life.

Chapter 4

WHEN DWIGHT OPENED the van door four hours later, Elenda didn't bother trying to hide her ordeal. She could have taken a shower or even changed out of her sweaty clothes at the hospital. Her mother's expert training and top of the line cosmetics likely would have hidden how pale Elenda was. None of those things mattered more than getting upstairs and off her sobbing legs.

"You okay, Elenda?"

"I've been better, Dwight. Has the pharmacy delivery made it?"

"Upstairs already. First physical therapy?"

Far from being proud and stubborn, she nodded, took both his hands, and let him pull most of her weight up. Her back joined in the chorus of agony. The shuttle driver met them with both sets of her crutches, the original full-length ones and a shorter set.

Now that she was only wearing a leg brace and well on her way to recovery, shorter crutches would be enough. So said the cruelest physical therapist to ever walk the earth on perfectly healthy legs.

"Let me help you upstairs," Dwight said, waving another car forward.

"I'd rather you didn't. I have to get used to it. Besides, I stink like a goat at the moment. If someone could bring those short crutches up later, that would be a huge help."

He frowned, but one of the more demanding residents was already headed his way. Elenda put on her best fake smile and moved slowly through the side door.

Her fantasies of a smooth and easy recovery, made possible by years of climbing so many stairs, dissolved when the cast came off. Those huge and strong leg muscles had wasted far more than she'd expected, especially in her pale, scrawny right leg. She'd managed not to cry at the sight, but only barely. She'd cried openly through the stretching exercises that followed.

Elenda made it to the elevator without anyone speaking to her, and she barely glanced up as the doors opened on an empty car. She was so grateful and exhausted that she stepped inside and pushed the button for the top floor without wondering who'd called it.

For the first time since she'd gotten tall enough, she didn't avoid looking out that diamond shaped window as the car moved. Elenda wasn't focusing on anything besides the blessed opiates waiting in her parents' apartment.

She'd habitually avoided looking out at the passing floors, but Elenda was sure she would have noticed a mirror replacing the clear glass.

A pale, drawn reflection stared back at her. Elenda was horrified at the dark circles under her eyes and lines around her mouth. Her hair was even faded, as if she'd gone gray since leaving that morning. She reached toward her hair, then froze.

The woman in the mirror moved too.

She didn't touch her hair, and she certainly wasn't still and staring.

Instead, Elenda's reflection covered her face with her hands. She seemed to be crying.

Elenda backed against the wall, whispering no over and over again.

The reflection continued to sob.

The bar pressed sharply against her aching lower back. Her heart pounded, and fresh sweat covered her body. One of her crutches crashed to the floor.

The woman in the reflection jerked her hands away at the noise, staring intently into Elenda's eyes.

Before she managed to force enough air into her paralyzed lungs to scream, the door opened. She bolted out, not caring what floor she was on, kicking the crutch as she went.

Elenda would crawl up the stairs if she had to.

She hit the wall hard enough to knock her multi-great grandfather's portrait off the wall. The heavy oval wooden frame hit the carpet, but the curved glass didn't break. Liam O'Dowd still gazed out into a world a hundred years past his own death. Black hair parted down the middle, pale middle-aged face emotionless, as if determined to reject countless changes in and around the building he'd brought to life by the considerable force of his will.

"That did not happen," Elenda said in a flat voice.

The elevator door stood open for what seemed like an eternity before it finally closed. As it dropped, she saw her own blue eyes in that tiny window. Red-rimmed, tear-streaked, and staring.

Chapter 5

THE LAST THING Elenda wanted was to make the long, painful journey down the quiet hall to her parents' empty apartment. Her original plan of taking two of her new pills so she could escape from pain into sleep felt like the worst idea she'd ever had.

One of the many reasons she'd hated that elevator so, and refused to ride in it from the time she was nine, was the horrible nightmares. She never knew if she'd be dropped hundreds of feet, shot miles into the air, caught in a vast space with dozens of oblivious passengers, or squeezed by shrinking walls until her racing heart woke her.

She'd felt the car jerked sideways or backward, the brass under glass walls replaced with billowing loose fabric, barely enough to keep her inside. Sometimes not enough to keep her inside.

Constantly when she was little, and even as an adult when Elenda was too tired or stressed out, the moving brass cage in her family's building turned her sleep into torture.

Whether her own changed face in the window was a pain-induced hallucination or not, she couldn't stand those same nightmares intruding on her waking life.

Elenda turned left instead of right, picking up her crutch but leaving the portrait where it was. She'd have to deal with that later.

Her hands were shaking too badly to do anything but knock the glass against the wall and shatter the whole thing. She hobbled to the end of the hall and knocked on the heavy six-panel door before she could reconsider.

Before Elenda counted to ten, a small, white-haired woman opened the door.

"Oh Lendy dear! Such a wonderful surprise! Come inside, get off of your poor knee."

Elenda sighed when the door closed between her and the elevator. The layout of the apartment was as large and sprawling as the others on the top floor, with arched doorways, herringbone wood floors, and ten-foot ceilings accented with dramatic, hand-painted crown molding. Her grandmother's dark wooden furniture, much of it older than her seventy-two years, completed the feeling of stepping back in time.

"Come into the kitchen, you look a fright," the older woman said. "Have you brought that book I asked you about?"

"Oh, I'm sorry, Gram. I just got back from the doctor. I didn't have a chance to go down there."

Her grandmother smiled and waved her hands, then turned to start the teakettle.

"Good news from the doctor, I hope?"

"Great news. Everything's healing faster than they expected. Gonna take me a long while to build my leg back up, though."

"Well, you'll be safe and comfortable here," her grandmother said. She set out two dark green china cups and saucers, then filled another plate with ginger cookies. The kitchen was as cozy as the rest of the apartment was gracious, but touches like the traditional lace tablecloth from Ireland made it welcoming. "Safer than anywhere else in the world. That's why I wanted to show you the book from the capstone."

Elenda almost forgot about the horrifying reflection in the elevator. Almost.

"I'll try to get down there or have Dwight do it. How would a book make me safe?"

"No, dear, that won't do. It must be someone in the family,

preferably you. No one who's not descended from Liam O'Dowd has ever opened our capstone. It won't happen for the first time on my watch. Honey or sugar?"

"On your watch?" Elenda shook her head. "Honey, please. I'm not following you, Gram. Why can't anyone open the capstone? Surely the city has to get down there for inspections or something."

"They do inspect the building, of course," she said, sitting down with the tea. "Though they'll never find one as well-built as this these days. But they don't get into the capstone. Or the vault."

"I've never even been in the vault. I don't much like the basement. Or the elevator."

"I do remember that, dear," her grandmother said. "I didn't like it when I was a girl, either. I outgrew that fear, as we all do. Tell me, have you kept up with your language studies?"

A sharp knock at the door startled Elenda badly enough that she almost dropped her teacup. She'd been about to ask this sweet old woman, one of her favorite people in the world, what the hell her years studying dead languages had to do with anything, or how some mysterious book could keep her safe. Her grandmother was up and opened the door before Elenda could even pick up her crutches.

"What a nice surprise! Two of my favorite people in one afternoon. Your father is joining us for tea, Lendy."

Elenda's father stepped inside, closed his eyes for a second, and sighed. Thomas Murphy was tall and rangy, his graying blond curls tamed by a business haircut. He'd already loosened his tie and unbuttoned his shirt. Unlike his wife, he wouldn't be caught dead wearing formal clothes unless he was forced to.

"Hey Mom. Thank goodness, Lendy. Dwight said you had a tough morning and handed me a pair of crutches. I was a little worried when I found your pain pills but couldn't find you."

"Sorry, Dad," Elenda said. She tried to stand to give him more room, but he put a hand on her shoulder and walked around to the other side of the table. "I just wanted some company."

"I'm glad you got that cast off," he said, adding milk to his own tea. "How long for the physical therapy?"

"Forever and a day. Depends on how much pain I can take."

"Well, you've beat things like this enough times. You'll come through with flying colors."

"I was just telling her she's a lot safer here," her grandmother said. "It's being away from home that lets these crazy things happen to any of us."

"I do fine when I'm working," Elenda said, winking at her father. They'd joked about her grace and good luck out in the wilderness compared to her klutzy tendencies elsewhere. "It's when I play it safe that I break bones."

"That makes perfect sense." Her grandmother nodded as she sipped her own tea. "It's where you live that counts. How was your day, Tommy?"

Elenda listened to the two of them chatter, trying to ignore the growing aches while remembering the odd things her grandmother said. Dementia didn't seem to run in the family, unlike the occasional youthful breaks with reality that everyone joked uneasily about.

A few of her cousins, only a handful out of a huge group scattered across the country, had succumbed to that madness before they'd turned forty. No one had ever been as old as her grandmother before it struck. But her Gram's words simply didn't make sense. Better to be safe than sorry.

When her father touched her shoulder, Elenda realized she wasn't hiding her physical or mental discomfort nearly as well as she thought.

"Thank you for the lovely tea, Mom," her father said. "I think someone's ready for those pain pills."

"You're right, Tommy, she's pale as a ghost. You get home and rest, Lendy, take care of your leg. Maybe when you're feeling stronger we can go down to the basement together."

Her father moved to help Elenda stand, but he was watching his mother.

"Anything I need to know about, Mom? Have you been feeling bad?"

"No, no, nothing of the sort. I'm just worried about my grand-daughter. See you later."

Elenda remembered the portrait when the two of them passed by.

"Sorry about knocking this off," she said.

"Did you? It was on the wall when I got home, as usual." He grinned. "That thing's always falling off. No idea how it doesn't break into a million pieces, except Liam's insistence on keeping an eye on all of us."

The same huge foyer opened into her parents' apartment as her grandmother's, but almost everything else was different. Elenda detoured into the much larger, more modern kitchen to grab her pain pills, then took the quick hop down into the sunken living room. Her father followed a couple of minutes later with a glass of water and a whiskey for himself. He joined her on the silver and black sectional just as she arranged the pillows perfectly around, under, and behind herself.

She swallowed two of the pills, the kind she'd had right after the surgery that knocked her out in record time. She was willing to fall asleep now that someone was home. In fact, all she wanted to do was close her eyes and escape from her aching legs, the bizarre vision in the elevator, and all the rest for a little while.

Her father sorted through the absurd amounts of mail the Murphys got every single day, putting several neat piles in the usual place on her mother's desk. When he rejoined Elenda, he brought her back to her strange reality.

"You looked worried back there, at least until the pain got too bad. Something happen with your grandmother that I should know about?"

"You heard her talking about the vault in that awful subbasement," she said, yawning. "She seems to think something down there will keep me safe or something."

"Did she mention a book?"

"Yeah, she asked me about that on my birthday, too. I've never heard about any kind of a book, certainly not one hidden away like that. Do you know what she's talking about?"

Her father dropped his gaze, but he was smiling.

"I know the general idea, sure. I figured the time was coming. But that's not for me, Lendy. It never has been."

The pills were hitting Elenda like a solid black curtain. She'd taken them on a mostly empty stomach for that reason, but now she wished her thoughts were more clear.

"Now I don't understand what you're talking about, either."

"You will," he said. He covered her up to her chin with her favorite pink chenille blanket, kept out for this purpose since she'd returned. "Let me give you a rare bit of fatherly advice even though you're all grown up. Your grandmother's right. Focus on getting your leg stronger. You'll learn a lot from her when the time is right. There's no hurry at all now that you're home."

Elenda wanted to protest that she'd be leaving as soon as possible. She couldn't even force her eyes to stay open, her mouth to form words, her brain to make some kind of sense out of the past couple of hours.

She needed to... She had to ask her father another question. Again, something about that damn subbasement.

Opiates and exhaustion took it from her mind with the next breath.

Chapter 6

ELENDA TRIED her hardest to heed her father's advice to take it easy, relax, let her injuries sort themselves out. She knew she should listen to her doctors and to her slowly healing body. Another encounter with the elevator wiped out all of her best intentions barely a week later.

She'd tried riding with her eyes closed to avoid that mirror, window, whatever the hell it was. The low level nausea she always got with pain medication made that impossible, so Elenda stared at the wall, reading the less than reassuring safety instructions over and over.

Then the compulsion to look—to *know*—got the best of her.

The first reflection, on Monday, showed her with swollen and puffy eyes, wearing what was obviously a black dress of mourning. No sign of crutches, but all the signs of a devastating loss.

The next, before her Wednesday appointment, held a different angle, lower than the rest. Elenda sat in an elaborate, electronic wheelchair, her mother standing close behind. The arrangement did not look or feel as temporary as yet another injury and slow recovery.

A motorized chair that expensive said forever.

The last reflection, on the way down this Friday morning, held herself still in the wheelchair, with her parents and Dwight behind her. The small car was crowded with her family's belongings. This time all their eyes showed signs of recent and prolonged tears.

After each vision, she thought of asking her grandmother or even her father about what she saw. And her fear of that fake smile she'd seen on her relatives' faces when her afflicted cousins came up in conversation kept her from saying a word.

Seeing that sickly sweet expression directed at her, about her, was more than she could stand to imagine.

When she returned from another painful PT session, Elenda convinced the driver she needed the walk with everything going so well. If the young man had been in that therapy room while Elenda trembled and sweated, he never would have agreed to let her out a block away. She moved as quickly as she could on the smaller crutches, the metal supports digging into her forearms.

Instead of heading to the main entrance and Dwight's protective gaze, she detoured down the cross street to the emergency exit. Compared to her recent habit of emailing her local friends and asking people at the hospital about short-term sublets, sneaking in the side door felt like a very small betrayal.

Some kind of change grew more important almost by the hour. Another three months of cowering in the elevator and avoiding her grandmother's odd requests would doubtless send her down the rabbit hole of insanity.

Her seldom-carried card key let her bypass the more public entrance, but rewarded her with an unplanned struggle to force the heavy steel door open. The stairwell that everyone, including the worried voice inside her own head, told her to avoid soared eight stories upward.

Pipes and wires, the building's life support systems, lined the concrete walls on two sides. The metal steps zigzagged against the other two, the handrails supported by steel uprights on the outside, anchored to the concrete on the inside. The vaguely chemical taste and smell of recent paint burned her eyes and lungs.

"Just take your time," she said under her breath. She held the right crutch under her left armpit. This part would certainly be easier without the longer version. "You've been up and down these a million times."

A million times. Yes.

With use of both legs, and with those legs conditioned to the task.

Elenda knew she'd made a mistake halfway up the second flight.

The problem wasn't only the strain of taking every step on one leg, already weakened from a long stretch of inactivity, then exhausted from her typical overzealous attack at physical therapy. It was more than her arms aching with the effort of pulling with her right and pushing with her left.

The problem was her balance. Every time she leaned on the crutch to lift her left leg, making sure not to put weight on her terribly weak right leg, she got more and more dizzy. Paint fumes amplified the effect. Her foot swung on an increasingly erratic pendulum, one that was eager to tip her backward and send her crashing down the dozens of concrete and steel ledges.

"Eleven more," she whispered, gritting her teeth, gripping the rail.

Elenda's heart pounded in her ears, and she smelled the oily sweat covering her body, increasing her chill in the cool stairwell. Turning around and going back down might be easier, but she was certain she'd lose her balance if she tried. She'd gone too far past her limits to reach her phone and call for help, even if she could get signal in this concrete tunnel.

Grunts with every step turned to groans.

Nine more steps.

Seven more.

Disaster struck three from the next broad expanse of concrete.

When she tried to force her exhausted thigh and hip muscles to drag her right leg up again, her toe caught under the lip of the step.

Pain from her wrenched knee tore through her. Elenda cried out, pulling her leg back, then screamed as her fragile balance deserted her.

She tried to grab the rail with her left arm, but the crutch caught on the step below and twisted her shoulder back. She landed hard on her left hip before tumbling down the stairs she'd so tortuously climbed, falling to the rock-hard landing.

She panted, too terrified to move. She'd fallen down stairs or off ramps or stages too many times to expect to be unhurt. But she'd been forced to remain still until an EMT could examine her neck and back many of those times as well.

If she'd managed to break a far more vital bone than she normally did, Elenda could do herself far more damage by trying to move on her own.

She was also one of the few residents who ever used these stairs, and had been for many years.

Her head had landed on her throbbing left shoulder, keeping her bruised skull from one more thump. She could see one of her crutches caught on the steps above, partly through the upright bars of the bannister. The other was under her ass. Sharp, jagged pain sang out from cuts and scrapes all over her face, arms, and hands. The impending bruises, especially on her hip, promised to be spectacular.

The rising stench of her own urine finally got her moving. She'd pissed herself on the way down.

Elenda turned her head forward as gently as she could, hissing at strained muscles in her neck and shoulders. Her arms and legs were screaming too loudly for her to have broken her back, and they reluctantly responded to her commands to move. Shifting enough to reach the crutch let her know she'd likely cracked at least one rib.

She pushed herself upright against the cold wall and waited for her heart rate and breathing to slow. She then pounded on the steel door with her crutch, resulting in a most satisfying and annoying hollow boom.

Her rescue came not long after from the third floor.

Chapter 7

ELENDA WASN'T SURPRISED to see how her face looked in the hospital bathroom mirror when her parents picked her up the next day. The first unnatural elevator reflection had given her a lurid and detailed sneak-peak. The small diamond-shaped view hadn't revealed the reality of her strained neck and back, cracked ribs, and mild concussion.

"I don't understand what you were thinking," her mother said. "It could have been so much worse."

Elenda sat between them in the middle seat of the hospital shuttle, a young woman driving today. She hoped the usual driver hadn't been fired for letting her walk.

"I wasn't thinking anything, Mom. I just wanted to see if I could do it."

Marian turned to stare out the window, but not before blotting a tear with her monogrammed lace handkerchief.

As soon as the elevator in their building started moving, Elenda looked at the window. For the first time since she'd arrived, she saw only empty hallways followed by dark sections of floor. A hot, uncomfortable twist in her gut told her that didn't mean the whole bizarre ordeal was over.

Some sort of truce, fickle and brief, held sway.

When her mother turned right in her customary quick march toward their apartment, Elenda touched her father's shoulder.

"Dad, I have to ask you a really strange question. Keep in mind that I knocked myself silly yesterday."

"You sure did," he said, raising one eyebrow. "A performance you're not going to repeat. Hear me?"

She nodded, not the least bit upset by his gentle scolding. She deserved it, and probably more.

"I hear you, and I won't. Do you ever see a mirror in the elevator? In the little window?"

He took a deep breath and crossed his arms, leaning against the wall. Their multi-great grandfather loomed over his shoulder, frozen in time and eternal.

Instead of the fake cheer she was terrified of, her father's eyes were warm and a little sad.

"No, Lendy. I never have. It never worked that way for me."

She opened her mouth to speak before his words sunk into her medicated brain. Her stomach dropped even though she was standing on solid ground.

"For you?" she whispered. "Does it work that way for anyone?"

Her father smiled a little, then jerked his chin at the portrait.

"I understand it did for him, among other things. Sounds like it does for you, too."

"I don't understand anything anymore." Tears prickled Elenda's eyes and nose. "What does this mean?"

"It means you need to get settled and relax, let some of this sink in," he said. He matched her slow pace down the hall. "And that it's time for a nice, long talk with your grandmother. Soon as you're able. Agreed?"

"Agreed. She keeps saying I'll be safe here. If she can make that happen before I really do manage to break my neck next time, I'm ready to listen."

Chapter 8

ELENDA'S BATHROOM mirror was as familiar and ordinary to her as her own hands. She'd stood on that cool white tile, mouth fresh from brushing her teeth or skin damp from taking a shower, seeing herself in the rectangular reflection on the back of the door as long as she could remember.

Her perspective had changed, certainly, from a toddler who had to reach up to hold the counter, to an awkward, skinny teenager who despaired of ever having curving hips or breasts like her mother, to the not as curvy as she'd hoped woman who nevertheless didn't usually mind catching a glimpse of herself in photos or reflection.

Yet today the view was as strange as anything she'd seen in the diamond-shaped version in the elevator.

Bruises decorated her flesh like algae blooming on a stagnant pond. Black and purple and green, all over her arms and legs. The worst were concentrated across her hips and back, along with the worst of the new pain. Dark clots of blood from scrapes highlighted several of the bruises and brought color to otherwise unmarked areas of her skin.

Underneath the deeper flashes of color were pale, twisting scars contrasting with the dark red marks around her knee. Reminders of previous falls and surgeries. A living diagram of her life so far. And not every injury left a mark outside of her memory. Breaks healed with only a cast, sprains and strains that improved over time.

None of her accidents had ever happened in this building though. Even her grandmother had said she was safe here, and until a couple of days ago, she had been. Until she tried to make arrangements to move out again.

Her father seemed to believe whatever her grandmother wanted to tell her even though he wouldn't say what it was. That often-delayed trip to the subbasement finally felt more dangerous to avoid than to take. Elenda hoped to find out more about whatever secrets that damn elevator held as well.

She strapped the brace on her right leg, moving slowly to avoid hurting her cracked ribs. Her mother would have to help with her shoes, no way around that. But Elenda was relieved she didn't need help getting dressed today.

An hour later, a couple of the pain pills in her pocket just in case, she hobbled out into the hall just as her grandmother opened her door at the opposite end. Molly Murphy smiled, looking like a girl of eighteen about to set out on a great adventure. Elenda moved like an old, old woman to meet her underneath Liam's portrait.

"Oh sweetheart," her grandmother said, frowning when she got a closer look at Elenda. "My heart hurts to see you like this."

"Mine too, Gram. I hope we can figure out how to make it stop."

The older woman touched Elenda's arm.

"That will be up to you. Are you ready?"

"I don't know. I guess we'll find out."

Her grandmother took the brass skeleton key off the hook and slid it into the lock. She turned it to the right then pulled it back out. The down button glowed green instead of orange.

For the first time in over twenty years, Elenda wasn't afraid when she stepped into the elevator. The feeling of hot, clenching dread in her belly shifted to warm, fluttery excitement. This time her Gram turned the key a full rotation. All of the floor lights from the eighth floor to the basement turned red.

"How do we get to the subbasement?" Elenda said.

"Haven't you ever used the handle?"

"No, I was afraid to touch it."

"I was when I was your age. Now I think it's great fun."

The older woman pushed the handle forward, and the elevator dropped faster than it usually did. Elenda grabbed the rails, her crutches banging against the metal. She wasn't quite as fearless as she'd thought.

"I'm sorry, Lendy. I won't go quite so fast."

She winked, then eased back. Their descent slowed along with Elenda's heart. The chimes for each floor still sounded. She glanced at the window, hoping to see the empty floors. Her own face looked back, but all of the bruises and scrapes had vanished. She was tan and healthy, like she always was after leading a long hike or a ski trip. A secretive smile grew as she looked to her right. A tall, beautiful woman with stunning thick black hair stood beside her, her complexion a rich brown.

"Do you see things in the window, Gram?" As soon as the words were out, Elenda felt nearly as lightheaded as when her grandmother sent the elevator dropping like a rock.

"I used to." She glanced at the window, then turned back to Elenda. "When I was younger. I haven't seen anything but a window since your grandfather died."

Elenda closed her eyes, remembering the vision of herself in mourning clothes. Had she been seeing her Gram's death? And she still didn't know *why* any of this was happening.

"What did you see then?"

"I saw myself smiling again." Elenda must have let her dismay show a bit too much. Her grandmother laughed. "That sounds awful, I'm sorry. I mean I saw that I wasn't going to cry forever. I still miss him every day, but that was the first time I understood I'd feel better eventually. I did, too. What do you see?"

"Nothing good," Elenda said. "Not until just a few minutes ago, but that's gone."

She wished for the strange mirror thing for the first time. Instead the window showed their slow progress past the lobby, sinking through the basement and a sea of glittering parked cars. A filthy and somehow frightening bunch of ancient pipes gave way to swirling layers of what looked like gray and white bedrock.

"How deep does this thing go, Gram?"

"Don't worry, Lendy. Neither of us is ready for the gates of hell. Not just yet."

Chapter 9

As the elevator coasted to a stop more gently than it ever did on the floors far above them, the rocky shaft opened up into a small room made of that same stone. When her grandmother let go of the handle, the door slid open.

Elenda could only see a couple of feet into the absolute darkness. If someone called the car back up, they'd be trapped down here in the pitch black deep below street level.

That was the first thing that scared her more than getting into the elevator in a long, long time.

"Are there any lights?"

"Of course," her grandmother said. "Do hold the door until I turn them on, though. Even these fancy modern bulbs don't last forever."

She stepped out onto a stone floor, rough but perfectly flat. She reached to the left of the door, and Elenda heard a soft click. Several beautiful curvy Art Deco glass fixtures flickered to life along the ceiling made of the same glittering gray rock as the floor and walls. Elenda suspected the bulbs were modern fluorescents, but those lovely green and black trimmed shades had to have been down here for a hundred years.

"What is this place? It's not the subbasement."

Her grandmother retrieved the key, and Elenda stepped out. The lights were controlled by two ancient round plastic cylinders, the one at the top now pushed in. She watched her Gram turn the key in yet another lock, one full turn to the right.

"We're below that, down in the family vault," she said. "You can step away from the door, dear. I have the elevator locked."

Elenda realized she was still holding her hand in front of the door. She followed her grandmother less than ten paces to the far end of the room carved deep into the Manhattan schist bedrock. Along the wall to their left, a narrow wooden table with a black leather top sat with four matching chairs. A gleaming solid brass door, as plain as most other fixtures in the building were ornate, covered the wall in front of them. An engraved oval doorknob waited over the final keyhole.

"This key opens only one door," her grandmother said with a smile.

She pulled a long, thick gold chain out of her blue sweater, a chain Elenda remembered her wearing on special occasions. At the end was a skeleton key made not of brass, but of the same gold. The top of the key was a cluster of red, blue, and white flowers surrounded by green leaves, the informal symbol many of her family wore in various kinds of jewelry. Elenda had a lovely enamel version made into a pin herself. She'd never seen it rendered in what had to be rubies, sapphires, diamonds, and emeralds.

Before Elenda could worry that the gold would be too soft, her grandmother fitted the key into the lock and turned it three times to the right. She grasped the handle and pulled. The door, almost the width of the wall, swung back.

Far from the mysterious hiding place Elenda was imagining, the light revealed rows of what looked like ordinary safe deposit boxes. The smaller ones had typical locks, and they were labeled with numbers. Several of those smaller ones a few inches tall clustered around a larger one in the middle, easily two feet square, again adorned with the cluster of flowers in gold set into the brass. This one had no lock.

When her grandmother touched the handle on that central

drawer, every bit of Elenda's hair stood on end. She stepped back, letting go of her crutch to hold on to the table. Every cell in her body rose to full, uneasy alert.

The drawer opened smoothly, and Elenda's jaw dropped. A cylinder of pale green stone lay on black fabric in the middle, almost as thick as her wrist and nearly as long as her forearm. The smooth surface was covered with what she thought was ancient, archaic Irish, the various angled lines and dashes of the rudimentary alphabet. No wonder her Gram was asking her about keeping up with her language studies.

Ignoring the stone, her grandmother pulled out a leather book that had to be hand-bound. The stitches were neat and small, but more visible than in any factory-made book for well over one hundred years. This was covered in some kind of hide, smooth and dark brown as if it had passed through countless hands.

Pressed into that hide were ancient letters that confused Elenda for a second. She caught one shape, then another. She blinked as words older than the book moved into place in her mind.

"Legacy of the Land," she said in an airy voice.

"Exactly so," her grandmother said. She was beaming. "From the day you were born, I knew it would be you."

Chapter 10

Elenda sat in the chair her grandmother pulled out, relieved to get off her leg even as her brain was spinning into mush. The green stone joined the book on the table.

"I don't understand," Elenda said, trying to steady her breathing. "Me for what?"

"Long before Liam O'Dowd left Ireland with his family, before he or his father or great-grandfather were ever born, a pact was made." Gram sat and picked up the stone wand. She turned it from side to side. Crystals and inclusions flashed and glinted among the carved markings. "Drawn between the people and the land. Only a few families understood the rewards, and the risks."

"What was the pact?"

Elenda kept her hands folded in her lap to keep from grabbing the stone. She was certain she'd be able to work out the symbols given enough time. She was even more certain that wasn't the way this ritual or ceremony or whatever was happening was supposed to go.

"One of the descendants must stay on the land," her grandmother said. "As long as that happens, the family and the land will prosper."

"But we left Ireland."

"We did, and many millions besides us." Her grandmother put the wand down just out of reach and opened the book. She turned the pages carefully, but too fast for Elenda's rusty translation even as the primitive language shifted into Old Irish, then Gaelic. "The English didn't understand the bond between our families and the land they worked, or perhaps they didn't care to. When they decreed each plot would be divided among all the heirs, the promise was broken. And all fell into ruin."

The neat, close text on the thick vellum pages had given way to simple columns. The left column held a printed name, the right the same name signed and dated. Her grandmother turned a few pages before Elenda caught a date she could easily read.

"Is that the year 902? As in over a thousand years ago?"

"Some of these were copied from older scrolls and books, I believe," her grandmother said. "But the original signatures start well before our Liam and his family fled the great famine and starvation in 1849. He suffered as many did here, even after escaping Ireland."

"Then the building opened fifty years later."

"Liam and others of his generation learned how to survive, how to thrive in their strange new land." Gram was still turning pages, her finger tracing the signatures. "A handful of them had these stone wands, brought out at great risk to their families. The English damaged the magic, you see, but they could not destroy it."

"So the pact is with the building now?" Elenda said. Cold, hard chills ran all along her flesh, making the scrapes and bruises sing.

"The building and the bedrock all around us. You've been to several of these in New York and in other cities. Each one has some sort of vault like this that holds the wand and the record."

"I'm sorry, Gram," Elenda said, shaking her head. Her stomach knotted as if she were in the elevator, still waiting for them at the other end of the room. "I still don't understand what this has to do with me. I don't seem to be safe here anymore."

She turned, taking Elenda's hand. She traced a scar on the back of her wrist, avoiding the fresh wounds.

"Did anything like this happen while you still lived here? Before you went to college?"

"No. It hadn't happened here before, either."

"I hope you'll forgive me for asking," her grandmother said, smiling. "Did you make plans to leave that day? Or try to?"

"How could you know that?" Elenda said. She fought the urge to pull her hand away. No one at the hospital would know who her grandmother was, much less have reason to pass along Elenda's casual inquiries about other places to live.

"I did the same thing a few times," her grandmother said. "My bad turns weren't as spectacular as yours, but the meaning was clear. Leaving here was a bad idea. If I had, none of the rest of the family would have been able to stay."

"What, am I on this list or something?"

Chapter 11

Elenda's heart sped up as her grandmother turned the next page. The line of names stopped halfway down with Molly Donahugh Murphy and a flowery, looping signature. July 17, 1967.

"Not yet, Lendy. I wanted to tell you what I could first. Once your name appears, your fate is set."

"My *fate*?" Elenda pushed the chair back, the wood scraping across the stone, and picked up her crutches. "I'm not interested in being some kind of caretaker here. Dad loves this place. What about him?"

"The pact doesn't work that way," Gram said with a sigh. "We don't choose this place. This place chooses us. Sometimes I think that's part of the damaged magic. The building wants the ones who don't return the feeling."

"Well, I'm not going to sit around here and turn into some kind of throwback bitter old spinster."

But that image, the last one she'd seen. Elenda hadn't looked bitter. And that slow smile at the gorgeous woman beside her didn't exactly scream spinster. She'd never seen herself looking more healthy or happy.

"I wouldn't say I'm a spinster, dear," her grandmother said. Elenda was relieved she was smiling. "I had a thrilling life, before and after I settled here for good. I loved my life with your grandfather and our children. I had my work and traveled the world, much more than a lot of women my age did. I only had to return here when it was time to unpack. I grew to love living here over the years."

"What about those names?" Elenda pointed at the top of the page. "The ones that are crossed out? Did they get to make other arrangements? What are those dates?"

Her Gram's smile turned sad.

"They made other choices, the same as you're free to do. When they crossed their names out, another person took their place. The dates are when they died. All of them young. And all of them badly."

"You're not honestly telling me this damned building killed them?"

"I'm telling you the magic, the twisted, broken magic left by the English, upheld the pact. When they left, their immediate families went with them."

Elenda slumped in the chair, letting the crutches slip back to the floor. She'd seen that very thing, her parents leaving with their belongings.

And she'd seen herself in a wheelchair.

Permanently.

"So if I go..."

"The accidents will get worse, Lendy my dear," her grandmother said, tears in her eyes. "When I'm gone, your parents would have to leave as well. Probably before then. Something would happen to make it come about. A change in jobs, maybe another accident. One of your cousins would move into your place."

She took both of Elenda's hands. She tried not to flinch at her grandmother's soft touch on the scrapes on her palms.

"Don't test it again, please," her Gram said. "My heart breaks to see you hurt like this. I wouldn't be able to stand seeing you worse."

"My work, Gram," Elenda said. "I can't do what I love here. Not in the city. No one needs adventure sports here. They won't let me teach mountain climbing on the buildings, will they? Despite what my mother thinks, people aren't exactly lining up to learn ancient languages, either. I can't afford to live here even if I wanted to."

"No, you don't have to give that up. I never did. We traveled all over the world, sometimes for months. But this was always home. And the one listed in this book, bound by the pact, does not pay to live here. That's all laid out in a very modern contract on file in the building manager's office. This situation is not without its rewards to make up for your sacrifice."

"Sacrifice is right," Elenda said. She drew away from the table, not wanting to touch the book or the stone. "How do you even know it's me? Just because you want it to be?"

"I do want it to be, yes, because I see how much pain you're in. But I'd never wish this on anyone who wasn't ready. I can't override what the building wants. I can't overpower the pact. You told me earlier you see visions in the elevator window."

"I do, or I did. But I don't understand how that leads some kind of life sentence to stay here. One I did not choose or agree to."

"There's more than that, my dearest. You still have a choice, but not an easy one."

Her grandmother gestured toward the book, toward where the names stopped with her own. Or where they had.

Elenda's blood ran hot, then cold at the faint lines appearing on the page. The tall capital letters first, and she couldn't deny the E taking shape no matter how badly she wanted to.

"I can't do this, Gram," she said, pulling herself up out of the chair. She managed to keep from groaning. Her abused and sore muscles had gotten stiff in the cool air. "I love you, and I appreciate you trying to help. But this is beyond what I can handle."

"You can think it over, of course. All I ask is that you be careful, Elenda. I don't want you to have an even worse accident. There wasn't a whole lot of room to play with after this last one, was there?"

"Do you realize how you sound?" Elenda said, dismayed at how quickly she was furious. "You're telling me if I don't follow some ancient spell I'm not even allowed to read, this building will somehow kill me?

"I know exactly how it sounds," her grandmother said. She gazed steadily at Elenda, but she made no move to get up and join her. "My grandfather told me the same things, and I thought he was just as crazy. He admitted thinking his own mother was a loon when she told him. But all of us recognized the truth over time."

"And your reward was long and healthy life, right? And the ones who resisted didn't live long enough to tell the tale."

Elenda grimaced at the harsh and angry sound of her own voice, amplified by the stone walls. Her grandmother didn't deserve to be talked to like that. And yet she couldn't seem to stop herself.

"I can't say you have years and years to make your choice, Lendy. But nothing has to be decided right this second. I just dumped a lot into your mind. I'm sorry."

"No, I'm sorry, Gram," Elenda said, shaking her head. "I'm being awful to you. Whatever this is really about, you're only trying to help me. Come on, Mom will be worried about us."

The older woman replaced everything in the bizarre safe and closed the massive door. She turned the lights out, hiding all of the mysteries from sight. At least for a little while.

Elenda hoped forever, even though she knew in her aching bones that wasn't true.

Chapter 12

A couple of hours and a couple of pain pills later, Elenda waited in the small family dining room for her father to get home. Her mother had banished her from the kitchen, a place she was uncomfortable in under the best of circumstances. The crutches and her slow and awkward movement were too much for either of them to handle.

Her phone vibrated in her pocket, and for some reason a chill raced through her. This anxiety wasn't as simple as not wanting to be scolded for devices at the table like a teenager, or as complicated as an unwelcome message from one of her various exes.

This chill began and ended with the lingering pains in her body and her heart, both new and old.

Elenda's smile at hearing from one of her oldest friends faded with every line.

Sorry she didn't get back sooner. Yes, there is a sublet opening up, less than a mile away. Closer to the hospital. Short term lease no problem for a grade school hiking buddy.

And of course, Elenda had to decide right away. Within twenty-four hours, before the place went on the market. She put the phone on the table, then covered her face in her hands.

Right on time, as if her Gram had planned it that way.

Disgusted at such a nasty thought, she grabbed the phone and tapped out a quick reply. She hit the send button before she could change her mind.

Asking how much and what floor it was on couldn't possibly hurt a thing.

Another hour passed before she heard another phone ringing in the kitchen. Her mother had been back and forth several times, wondering and worrying what was taking Elenda's father so long. After a few minutes of quiet conversation, Marian joined her daughter at the table. Her face was pale and strained.

"What's wrong, Mom?"

"Everything's fine, Lendy." The lie could not possibly have been more obvious. "Your father will be home in a few minutes."

She refused to say more.

When Elenda's father finally came in, more than two hours late, he was a different man than the one who'd left that morning. His step was slow and heavy, and his face was nearly as pale as his wife's.

After a couple of minutes in the kitchen, the two of them joined Elenda at the table. Her mother's lashes were damp, her eyes red and puffy.

Elenda struggled to keep her face straight while her thoughts raced.

This is all my fault. Whatever it is, illness or some other disaster, this is all because I'm too stubborn to do what my grandmother wants me to do. I'm too stubborn to have a damn permanent address, no matter what it costs me or anyone else.

"Listen, I'm not sure this is going to come to anything," her father said. His voice and drooping shoulders said otherwise. "I may be getting transferred to our West Coast division."

"They swore this wouldn't happen, Tom," Elenda's mother said, tapping her fingers on the dark oak table. "Years ago. It's supposed to be in your contract."

"It is there, Marian. And sometimes these mergers get more complicated than we expect."

"Not permanently, right?" Elenda said. "Just for a transition or something?"

"I'm afraid not. If this thing goes through, our whole team goes. Most of them are even excited about it."

"And you're not, Dad."

It wasn't a question. The only question was whether Elenda could live with this any longer than she lived through another series of accidents.

"No, I'm not. I fought to get that into my contract for a reason." He took his wife's hand as he looked around the small room. Unlike the larger formal dining room, this one was lined with family photos and mementos. "I don't want to leave the city. I don't want to leave our home."

"I'm sure you can fight it," Marian said, a flash of color returning to her cheeks. "People don't have to just take these things anymore. You have options."

"Yeah, I suppose I do," he said. He scrubbed his fingers through his hair, leaving it standing in disorganized gray and blond peaks. "Not many good ones at my age, though."

"This will break Gram's heart," Elenda said, almost to herself.

"I'm worried about that too," her father said. "She's doing well, sure. But things like this aren't easy on young people, much less someone her age. Did you two get a chance to talk today?"

Elenda stared at her father, wishing she could transfer this whole thing to him. Let him be the one the building wanted. The one the damned pact wanted.

Even a line through her own name, through her own life, wouldn't make that happen.

"We did talk," she said, wiping tears away before her parents saw them. "I'd like to talk to you, though. Mom, too. Maybe not right now."

Elenda's mother placed her hands flat on the table, then got to her feet.

"I think this is the perfect time for you to talk," she said. She touched Elenda's shoulder, then her father's. "I'll get dinner warmed up."

Chapter 13

Elenda watched her mother leave. The radio in the kitchen clicked on, then got louder than Marian usually kept it. Pop music from Elenda's teen years, her mother's guilty pleasure known only to the three of them, created a fast-paced wall of privacy. When Elenda met her father's gaze, his eyes didn't look any less upset, but he was smiling.

"We don't have to do this now, Dad."

"We're both sitting right here. Your mother's making it clear she thinks it's time." He crossed his arms and leaned back in his chair, long legs stretched under the table. "I've never been more desperate for a change of subject."

A short bark of laughter, manic and strange, escaped Elenda's tight throat.

"It may not be a change of subject, not if Gram was telling me the truth." She drew in a shaky breath. "What do you know about the family vault? Down in the subbasement?"

Her father half smiled, raising his eyebrows.

"I know we have a bunch of paperwork in one of the deposit boxes down there. Wills, deeds, a few stocks. Nothing we need to get to all that often, but things I'd rather have here than at the bank.

I've never seen inside the big safe, Lendy, if that's what you're asking. I'm guessing your Gram showed you that today."

"Yeah, she did." Elenda ran her hands through her hair just before she realized she shared that habit with her father. "Am I... Does it break some kind of secret rule if I talk to you about this?"

"If it does, your grandmother and her grandfather before her broke that rule a long time ago. Bunch of the cousins did, too. I heard the tales of the book, the legacy book. She told me I'm not in there, no matter how much I always wanted to be. Still true?"

"Still true. I wish you were instead of me. Is this why you might get transferred, Dad? Because of me?"

He shrugged.

"This is where your grandmother might know more, but I doubt she does. No one seems to have all the answers, at least no one alive. Her theory on why you keep getting hurt is because you resisted the fate you were born to. Does that make sense to you?"

Elenda rubbed her aching eyes.

"Well, the timing fits, anyway. I'd asked around about sublets before I had my little accident in the stairwell. Earlier that same day. Then today, after Gram took me down to the vault, I heard back about one. As soon as I replied and said I was interested, you called Mom."

"If anyone else told me that, anyone outside the family, I wouldn't believe a word of it. But coming from you, and about this, I'm afraid to *doubt* a word of it."

He sat forward and took one of Elenda's hands into his own cold ones.

"This isn't something you can be forced into, Elenda. I don't think it works that way, but even if it did, I'd never want that."

"What if it is why you're getting transferred? You wouldn't want—"

"No. I would not. I doubt my mother agrees with me, but I would much rather you make your own choices, live your own life, instead of making yourself miserable staying here."

Elenda surprised herself by smiling.

"Gram said the building wants the ones who don't want to live here. Like a cat knowing which person does not want a lapful of cat hair."

"That's just what I've always heard, but not put so well. We all talked among ourselves, long before we understood what we were talking about. The cousins, nieces, nephews. Everyone who wasn't chosen, the ones who were. Some like me who wanted this, others who were scared to death it would be them."

"Like me," Elenda whispered.

"Maybe so. I think my generation got a lot more quiet and secretive before any of you were born. You didn't have a bit of warning, did you?"

"Not even a hint. Not until Gram started asking me about the vault."

"I'm sorry about that, sweetheart, I truly am. I don't know why all of us changed at once. Maybe paranoia about causing bad luck somehow. Maybe fear of the government finding out and making us pay taxes or something. You know all that conspiracy theory nonsense that went around back then. Hell, maybe something to do with our whole culture changing, people moving around so much more than they used to. Whatever the cause, it wasn't fair to you or anyone else your age."

"Oh, I don't know. If I had known, do you think I would have ever come home? You might not have seen me a single time after high school."

"Listen, seriously, don't make a decision you're going to regret. Not because of me, and not because of your grandmother."

"You know what else Gram said, Dad? She said that was why I get hurt so much, why my accidents keep getting worse. Did she tell you about the people who did decide to ignore all of this and leave anyway? What happened to them?"

He closed his eyes and turned away.

"I went to their funerals. Visited a couple in facilities. I never knew for sure, but we all suspected how they got that way. *Why* they got that way. I'm sure she showed you the book. I'd be willing to bet the crossed out names match up with all those early deaths, or the ones who lost their minds."

"So you know what could happen to me. Choice or not, this truly is life or death." Elenda waited until her father looked back at her and nodded. "How much does Mom know about all of this?"

"Only the general idea. How someone in the family always stays with the building, just like on the land that's left back in Ireland. She knows it's not me, but that because it is my mother, our rent is a tenth of what anyone else would pay. I don't have to tell you how much she loves living here. For what it's worth, though, she wouldn't want you to be forced into anything, either."

Elenda gazed around the room, at the photos all over the walls. Mostly of her and her parents, though her grandmother was in quite a few. She couldn't imagine any of them living anywhere else, not any more than she'd ever seen herself living here for the rest of her life.

She hadn't imagined living here even one more day after she left for college with no intentions of looking back.

"I don't know how to make a decision like this, Dad. I never really have, you know? The longest lease I ever signed was six months, and I hated the place from that day until I got away. Even that's longer than my longest relationship."

Her father snorted softly, smiling at the same time.

"That part I can't help you with. I have no doubt you'll meet the right person when you're ready." He let go of her hand, sat back, and sighed through his lips. "I can't really help you with the rest, either. I want you to be safe, sure. It rips my heart out to see you hurt like this. I want you to be happy, too."

"Back to square one." Elenda smiled to soften her words. "Does all this new secretiveness mean you don't know anyone my age who's signed on for this? Someone I could talk to?"

"I have my suspicions. This is another question for your grandmother, Lendy. I don't know if anyone keeps central records or anything like that, though it would make sense. I'm sure she knows everyone else in the city. Probably all along the East Coast. I wouldn't be surprised if she knew a lot more."

Elenda nodded, wondering if her grandmother would only give her names of people who were happy with the arrangement. When the radio in the kitchen snapped off, she jumped hard enough to cause a knotting spasm through her wrenched back.

If the next fall would be worse than this, anything her grandmother said, anyone Elenda talked to, may not make any difference.

Chapter 14

THE VAST CAFETERIA-STYLE restaurant in the East Village was less crowded than usual in the brief hours between the lunch and dinner rushes. Elenda had arrived earlier than she meant to. The mostly Eastern European staff didn't mind to hold the table, happy to have a chance to slow down and chat with her. Colorful murals decorated the walls, and Old World comfort food and a dizzying variety of pastry waited to settle the nerves fluttering around in her belly.

As soon as Elenda's grandmother had given her the list, much longer and covering far more of the world than her father suspected, the decision of who she most needed to talk to was clear. Her cousin Rick lived down in Washington, DC, where he was born, but he and his family had often visited New York when he and Elenda were young. She remembered a moody, distant boy who never seemed to fit in.

Her youthful self couldn't resist the challenge of another outsider, and the two became close friends. Elenda hadn't seen Rick for a while, but she'd heard stories about his rising and falling fortunes. Some of those stories included treatment for serious depression, but not for a few years now.

Elenda knew her old friend would tell her the truth. Rick cooperated by immediately agreeing to take the train up for a visit.

She recognized him as soon as he walked in the door. The skinny, pale boy with thick glasses and floppy brown hair had vanished along with the gaunt, shadowed look of his teenaged years. Rick exuded comfort in the space around him, in his clothes, in his skin. The handsome man who lit up the room with his smile when he saw Elenda had moved beyond finally fitting in. Rick now had a deep, natural confidence that spread to everyone around him.

"You look fantastic, Lendy, crutches and all!"

"Well, better than I did a few weeks ago for sure." Elenda ignored the metal appendages and she stood just in time for his hug. "You look wonderful, Rick. Something's been treating you right."

He rolled his eyes and shook his head, a habit Elenda remembered well.

"I think maybe I finally grew up. Happens to all of us if we live long enough. Now tell me how the hell you broke yet another bone, cousin?"

The catch-up talk lasted through a delicious and generous Ukrainian meal and decadent round of sweets before Elenda ran out of time. She'd almost managed to convince herself this was nothing but a long-overdue visit, or maybe a successful young writer gathering material for a comedic story about her spectacular run of bad luck. Not a far more sinister interview about a topic she was afraid made her sound crazier than it made her feel.

Rick was gentle about it, but he yanked her back to reality quite effectively.

"So I hear through the usual channels that you may be rejoining us on the East Coast?" he said, one eyebrow raised.

"And what channels are those?" Elenda tried not to laugh, but it was a losing battle. "I haven't decided anything just yet."

"You already talked to Auntie Kay, my dear Lendy. You know she didn't want someone else to scoop her with news that big."

This time it was Elenda's turn to roll her eyes.

"What does she have, some kind of phone tree set up?"

"Something like that. She might even have her own app by now. Listen, I'd be the last one to dig into your business if you don't want me to. I know you called me for a good reason. I have a good idea what it is, too, but I want you to tell me."

Elenda let out a long breath through pursed lips. She'd almost forgotten how direct and no nonsense Rick could be. Again, exactly what she needed to get herself talking in a case like this.

"If you talked to Auntie Kay you already know why, don't you?" He shrugged, leaving her no choice but to spill it. "My grandmother, she's not sick or anything, but she's been talking to me about where I might want to live next. Or where I might have to, if I know what's good for me for a change."

Rick nodded slowly, not quite smiling.

"Sounds familiar. That's pretty much how it finally hit me. Only I didn't have your habit of collecting broken bones. I was well on the way to breaking my mind, though."

"When you lived somewhere else, right?" Elenda said, the hair on her arms standing up. "But when you went back home, it got better?"

"Exactly right. I'm not sure if our family is lucky or cursed. No one tells us we're wasting our time with jobs like writing or leading extreme outdoor adventures or all the other weird things we get into. But if some of us decide to move out on our own, all hell breaks loose."

Elenda watched his brown eyes, afraid to interrupt now that he was talking. Her Auntie Kay had been all positive and excited, full of nothing but stories of how wonderful her life was. How wonderful Elenda's life would be once she got settled in.

Just as Elenda had suspected, Rick's experience sounded a lot more like her own.

"I'm sorry to drag all of this up," she said. "I just...I wanted someone to be honest with me instead of trying to sell me on the idea, you know?"

"I do know. I'll tell you the truth whether you really want it or not, on one condition."

"Name it."

"If you do decide to stay on this side of the country, we don't go ten years between visits ever again."

Elenda laughed, more tension than she'd realized leaving her body in an instant. Even if all of it came right back, she was grateful for the reprieve.

"You got it. You can stay with me, and my grandmother will spoil you stinking rotten."

"I'll hold you to that. I could use a good dose of Molly's spoiling." Rick waited for the waiter to refill both of their teacups, staring at Elenda the whole time. He didn't speak until she nodded.

Chapter 15

"So I GET out of college, all prepared to write my Great American Novel. Or at least the novel that sold a ton of copies. You already know that first one *did* sell well. Probably too well. Once I started seeing steady income and got a contract for the next two, what was my gift to myself?"

"You moved to New York. Just like writers are supposed to."

"Of course. That was almost a requirement of the book deal. And everything gradually fell to pieces. I got the next two books out, yeah. The few people who read them raved about how much better they were than the first. And no one else bought them. Not until some asshole decided to claim the third one as his own."

"I'd forgotten about that! I was already out West collecting those broken bones. You ended up in court for a while, didn't you?"

Rick picked up his heavy white tea mug, turning it between his hands and breathing in the bergamot-scented steam.

"Three years with all the paperwork and continuations and nonsense. Long enough to eat up everything I'd earned and send me down into the pit inside my head for even longer. He finally tripped himself up when they forced him to testify, but the damage was done. I knew I'd never plagiarized a word from him or anyone else, and he finally had to admit it. That wasn't nearly as exciting a story, though, so not many other people heard the outcome.

"I moved back home to get my head on straight, and to try to get out of the financial mess. I hadn't written much during all that time. Partly paranoia about another lawsuit, justified or not. Mostly depression. I assumed moving back into the same old building in the same old city I'd grown up in would put me in the hospital, but I didn't see any other choice. Just the opposite happened. I was writing, feeling better, and even those first three novels started selling again."

"Miracle cure, huh?" Elenda said. "I heal up so fast here that the doctors can't believe it. At least until I manage to fall down a few flights of concrete steps."

Rick winced, closing his eyes for a second.

"You know, I've thought several times I'd give anything to have this affect my body instead of my mind. It would suck just as bad, wouldn't it? Anyway, when my fourth novel came out, all was forgiven. They were talking TV pilots, maybe a movie. So what did I do again?"

"Same thing I did, of course. Finally move out on your own so you can start your life."

"Like normal people, right?" Rick's voice was low, bitterness making Elenda's heart ache. "That was the biggest joke of all from the day we were born. That time my great escape was heading out to Los Angeles. I figured a real change of scenery would do me good. When all the deals fell through, I ended up in the psych ward for a couple of months. Want to guess what happened next?"

Elenda shook her head. She didn't want to guess, and she really didn't want to hear more. And this kind of tale, once started, had to be finished.

"Same thing that happened to me not that long ago," she said. "Your parents wanted to take care of you and help you recover, so back you went."

"They really were great. My parents, I mean. They weren't trying to force me into anything either way. My mother knew the history of crazy floating around our gene pool as well as we all do. And I did recover. Even got a couple of novellas and a bunch of short stories out into the world."

"What kept you from heading out into the world again?"

"My own version of your grandmother. My grandfather caught me aside when I started talking about moving. I think my mother clued him in. To tell you a truth I haven't admitted to anyone else, I was already pretty clear on the pattern, and terrified that I'd never be able to break out of it. So I was ready to listen."

He picked at the remains of poppy seed cake.

"I'm not saying I regret my decision. These last seven years have been the best of my life in a lot of ways. But I do wish I'd been a bit more clear-headed when I made it. I've been through anger at my mother, my grandfather, and most of all myself for not taking the time to truly understand what I was doing. I also knew if I waited, if I instead decided to test the depths of my lurking insanity, that I probably wouldn't make it out at all.

"So I signed the little book in the basement, probably a hell of a lot like the one you've seen by now. I can't say I've never looked back or wondered what would have happened if I'd left anyway, but I'm still there." He tapped his temple. "And I'm still here."

"Do you ever wonder what would happen if you did change your mind, Rick? If you just decided to move out even after you signed?"

"Don't have to wonder." He smiled, but it was tight and humor-less. "A few people have done just that. The last a couple of years ago in Chicago. Her name was Cassie. Most of them have killed them-selves within a few months. A few have been locked up for good. Cassie did both and managed to off herself in the hospital."

Elenda rubbed her eyes with both hands, squeezing until purple lightning filled her vision. Her eyeballs ached and the afterimage lingered when she met Rick's gaze.

"So you're telling me to-"

"No no, none of that. All I'm telling you is what happened to me. Our family is actually a good bunch despite our unique situa-tion of luxurious indentured servitude. But you're one of my favorites even in a mostly likable group. I'd be sad if something worse happened to you, Elenda. But I'd respect your decision no matter what. I respected Cassie even though I knew what would happen. Partly because she did too, and she did it anyway."

He leaned forward and lowered his head, looking up into Elenda's eyes.

"All I'm telling you is make sure you know what you want. Don't rush into anything. This legacy had us maybe before we were born, but once you sign that book, it's for life. A very long life, too, judging by everyone I've met since I joined the club. So *make sure.*"

Elenda watched a group sitting nearby, all of them speaking a language she couldn't understand. Those words sounded as odd to her ears as the ancient Irish and other languages she knew would sound to almost everyone else in the city. They'd possibly left home and family behind with no real expectation of ever seeing them again.

New York was full of people who'd fled awful situations Elenda didn't want to imagine.

All that uncertainty, fear, and sacrifice for the chance at a new life.

The same thing Liam O'Dowd had given her family over a hundred years ago.

"Do you have a portrait in your building, Rick? The first one from your family who left Ireland?"

"You mean our Eternal Hall Monitors?" He snorted. "They're there, sure. A floor below mine, but close enough. Robert and Katharine Sullivan were more all-seeing than Santa to my young self. I remember yours, opposite that creaky old elevator, right?"

"One of the reasons I never much liked that elevator. Liam O'Dowd knows exactly who comes and goes, probably in the whole building. Listen, Rick, do you have to get back right away? Or can you stay for a couple of days? I have a thousand questions, if you're willing. And I'll be selfish and admit I just want to talk to someone my own age about all of this."

Rick's smile erased her pain and confusion, and years of his own fell away from his face. They were two weird kids hiding out from all the normal people all over again.

"Ask me anything you can think up, cousin." He leaned forward, looking into her eyes and grinning like the devil himself. "Do you have any idea how many times I've wanted to rewrite all of this for myself? How rarely anyone actually *gets* that chance? I'll do anything in my power to make sure this is on your own terms, for your own reasons. Then I'll toast your success and independence no matter what you decide. Deal?"

Chapter 16

Elenda didn't feel the chill, in the air or in her bones, nearly so much the next time she stood beside her grandmother in the family vault. Several people joining them warmed up the bedrock space more than she expected. A couple of weeks passing had let her body heal enough to not be nearly so achy and sore.

The main difference was the warmth in her heart. A settled, secure warmth. She didn't quite trust that sensation, one she'd never felt here or anywhere else in her entire life. But she enjoyed the solid comfort nonetheless.

The short crutches waited in the corner beside the elevator, but Elenda was relieved to stand on her own as her grandmother opened the massive vault door once again. Rick stood with her Auntie Kay and another cousin she'd spoken to in a row behind her, her father on Rick's other side.

Their words and stories of how their lives had changed since they'd accepted the legacy of the family land wouldn't have been enough to change Elenda's mind on their own.

Not if all of them had been glowing and positive, anyway. Physical, financial, emotional, none of the mysterious incentives were exactly the same. Elenda didn't doubt the challenges they told her of were true, though, and exactly what would be most effective in every case.

None of them were dressed formally by New York City standards, but blue jeans and t-shirts had no place on a day like this. Elenda wore a dark blue ankle-length dress that coordinated with her grandmother's pale blue suit. The older woman turned slowly, holding the heavy green stone wand as if it were light as a feather. Eyes bright and cheeks glowing, she looked at least twenty years younger.

"Elenda Margaret Murphy. The land has need of a steward. A protector. One to watch over and provide for. An exchange of love and sacrifice."

Elenda's grandmother stepped forward, still holding the stone close to her body.

"That sacrifice demands a choice, though it offers great reward. You must choose freely. You must understand the seriousness of the bond you make with magic older than the country we call home."

"I understand," Elenda said. "I choose freely and with my own will."

"Then, my dear granddaughter, we welcome you."

Elenda took the wand carefully, surprised at how warm it felt. The heat didn't come from her grandmother's hands, not with the whole length and breadth of green rock as long as her own forearm. That much warmth could only come from within.

Her grandmother turned back to the vault and brought out the leather-bound book. She opened it on the table, turning the page to the last line of signatures and dates. Elenda wasn't at all surprised to see her own name fully formed.

"As you must choose with your own mind and heart," her grandmother said, "you will sign with your own hand. As it has been since time too distant to measure."

Elenda was confused when her grandmother pulled an ordinary black ballpoint pen out of her breast pocket. A rather nice Cross model, of course, no disposable junk for Molly O'Dowd Murphy. But none of the long, arching ostrich plumes, solid gold fountain pens, or dire instruments for extracting her blood that she'd imagined.

The older woman winked when Elenda shifted the stone wand to her right hand and took the overwhelmingly normal writing instrument. She stepped back, leaving Elenda alone with the book.

Sudden trembling threatened to overwhelm her still-weak legs. Elenda sat, closing her eyes to let a thousand questions flash through her mind. More than a thousand, and more than her own lifetime's worth.

But for her, and in this lifetime, all of the questions came down to only one answer. One she never would have believed even a few short days ago, but now Elenda made the decision for herself, free and clear.

As she formed the swirls, lines, and angles of her own name, the settled, comfortable warmth moved out from her heart. Her belly, her throat, her legs, even her fingers took on the inner glow.

The sensation was strongest in her left hand, curled over the stone wand on the table beside her. A sharp, high scratching, heard more with her fingertips than with her ears, kept pace with the softer scratch of pen across paper. Elenda's left palm grew hot enough that she was afraid she'd have a blister to go with all the rest of her healing wounds, but she kept her hand still.

The stillness felt right, somehow.

Elenda put the pen down and raised her left hand at the same moment. On the paper to her right, the date took shape beside her signature, black letters floating up from the pale surface.

On the wand, a far more primitive signature glowed before shifting to the same paler green of the other markings. A flat line like a table, with five diagonal lines underneath. Elenda didn't recognize that word, not from the original artifacts, anyway. She knew if she studied the stone, though, perhaps compared with the signatures above her own in the ancient book, she'd find more breadth and depth to the primitive language than she or any other scholar had suspected.

She got almost gracefully to her feet and turned right into the arms of her grandmother.

"Welcome, my dearest, my darling girl," she whispered. "The land welcomes you home."

Chapter 17

Later that same day, Elenda couldn't stop staring at the view from her new apartment. Even in a building she'd lived in or come home to throughout her life, she'd never suspected a vista so custom-made for her own eyes, mind, and heart.

The trees, grass, water, and stone of Central Park didn't take up the whole horizon, but the stretch she could see was enough to settle her wanderlust for the moment. Even with a crowd swirling behind her on the huge patio space, when Elenda leaned her elbows against the gray stone pillar and focused on the park, she could pretend no one else was anywhere around her.

Behind her, several strides away from the edge of her outdoor paradise, the building rose straight up to the roof, with the setback giving her nearly as much room outside as in. The previous tenant had taken advantage of the space and the sunlight with several garden boxes scattered around the area.

Almost all of them were empty now with autumn coming on and the family leaving, but Elenda thought she would continue the garden herself. With room for climbing plants against the building and several other levels and arrangements all around her, growing her own food could be another way of making herself at home.

A soft footstep behind her brought Elenda back to the reality of ignoring her own apartment-warming party. She picked up her drink and turned to rejoin the festivities.

"This is a beautiful view," her mother said. "I'd never been down here before you decided to move in."

Marian wore her usual dark blue pantsuit, but she'd added a scarf and jewelry in the same lighter shades as Elenda and her grandmother wore. The choice of apartment wasn't one she approved of, and she'd worked very hard to keep that to herself. Elenda gave her mother full credit for what had to have been a difficult effort. Even with the reality of none of the top floor family apartments being available, she knew her mother thought she should just live at home until one opened up.

"I had no idea you could see the park from here," Elenda said. She inspected the garden and flower boxes, some still vibrant with greens and colorful autumn flowers. "I think I may have to take up gardening, believe it or not. Maybe you can help me figure out what to do with this stuff once I grow it."

Their eyes met, and both women smiled. Elenda knew in her heart that the one floor separation between them would make all the difference in the world, in the best way.

"Nothing brings more joy to a city dweller's heart than fresh produce and flowers." Elenda's mother ran her fingertips through a tight bundle of deep red mums. "I'm sure we can work out what to do with anything you grow."

The setback between floors was deep enough to let about twenty people wander around, with a few more sitting inside the nearly empty apartment. Several family members who hadn't been part of the ceremony had joined them for the late afternoon party, almost like a wedding reception after the service.

Elenda laughed under her breath, thinking this situation wasn't all that different.

"I could use a little help looking for furniture, too," she said. "I've never had much more than would fit in a few suitcases."

Her mother's eyes lit up, and she tilted her head.

"Well, we have plenty down in storage, but you already know

that. If any of it suits you, it's yours. Otherwise we'll find exactly the pieces you love most."

Delia, one of Elenda's friends who'd been on that life-altering - and knee-shattering - trip to Colorado, broke away from the group in front of the open door. When Elenda started to wave her friend over, her mother grabbed her hand. Before Elenda processed her surprise at such an impulsive action from proper Marian Murphy, her mother's words drove it from her mind.

"Nothing on earth would make my heart happier than to have you home, Elenda. But I don't want your heart broken. Are you sure about all of this? Are you happy?"

"I'm not sure about anything. This whole thing hasn't give me much time to think, not that too much time to think ever works out well for me. I am happy, Mom. I didn't miraculously turn into a homebody overnight, no. Being back in the city will take some getting used to. But I'm happy."

The two women hugged tight, and Elenda kissed her mother's cheek.

"That's all I need to hear," Marian said. "Welcome home."

A stubborn irritation in her eyes, very much like tears, kept Elenda blinking furiously. She watched stuttering stop motion as her mother turned away, paused to hug Delia, and kept moving. By the time Delia's dark brown streaked with purple hair swam into view, Elenda had herself more or less under control.

"Quite the setup you have here, Ms. Murphy. No roommates, either?"

"No one at the moment. It is nice not to be desperate and begging someone to move in for a change."

Delia turned in a slow circle, her bright blue eyes taking in every detail as they had since the two of them met on a grade school hiking trip. One of the good things about moving back to the city would be visiting more friends scattered across the boroughs rather than across the country. Delia's message about a sublet close to the hospital, and the almost immediate call from Elenda's father, had set countless unseen wheels in motion.

"I'm not even going to ask what kind of crater this place made in your bank account," Delia said. "I've never known you to even have a year-long lease, and now you own a view several million people would kill for."

Both women leaned against the just over waist high stone wall facing the park.

"It wasn't as bad as you'd think, Dee. I'm sure I'll take a while to get used to the city again, but I think this will make a good home base."

Delia leaned forward, wavy hair falling into the breeze. Elenda hoped she'd eventually come to trust the compact she'd made with the land and the wand as much as she trusted the iron-clad but ordinary contract she'd signed in the business office. Even if her physical accidents stopped, she doubted she'd ever have the same dancer's confidence as her friend. Delia rose to her toes, shoulders pushed far past the boundary.

Right before Elenda gave up her struggle to keep from yanking her friend onto more solid footing, Delia straightened, flipped her hair back, and caught Elenda in a quick hug.

"I say you've had more than enough bad luck over the years, Lendy. If coming home changes all of that for you, maybe that tumble back in Colorado was worth it."

Chapter 18

Three months later

CLIMBING out of a taxi with no help at all - from crutches, leg braces, or another person - was a miracle Elenda was determined to remember. Even after three glorious weeks of summertime mountain climbing in Chile, stepping out onto a freezing New York City sidewalk under her own power delighted her. Dwight's broad smile only reinforced how much progress she'd made over the past few months.

"You look great, Lendy," he said. The junior doorman was already gathering her bags to take upstairs. "Had a good trip?"

"Fantastic trip, Dwight. I finally feel like myself again."

"Well, you look like a million bucks. Glad to see you home safe and sound."

Elenda tried to keep her rueful smile to herself as she walked across the green marble lobby. After a few weeks away, the place did look good to her eyes. And that odd settled comfort in her belly welcomed her home.

The elevator door opened as soon as she walked up to it, as it often had since she'd held that stone wand and recited the words written upon it. She paused for a second, tempted to head to the stairs and continue building her legs back up.

May as well get used to this, especially if the silly thing was going to give her special treatment.

As soon as she stepped inside, a woman's voice called out from behind her.

"Hold the elevator, please!"

She grasped the door and leaned out.

A lovely woman with rich brown skin and long curly hair walked as fast as she could with a suitcase and a backpack. Elenda immediately felt guilty about Dwight and his assistant dealing with her travel bags. She pushed the door open button and grabbed the suitcase.

"Thank you so much," the woman said, panting. Under her coppery winter coat, she wore an ankle length burgundy skirt and a paler shirt that somehow made the flush in her cheeks even more appealing. "This thing can take a while if you miss it."

"No worries at all. What floor?"

"Seven."

As the door closed, Elenda caught her perfectly normal reflection in the glass. Her tanned face, her own cheeks flushed from the sudden cold, her bright and happy eyes. Warmth flooded through her as she recognized the scenario. A perfect recreation of the vision she'd seen in the elevator the first day she'd visited the vault with her grandmother.

For a second, fast enough that she wondered if she imagined it, she saw her multi-great grandfather instead of the floors moving past. He stared right into her eyes. His serious, stony expression transformed into a warm smile, every bit as lovely as her father's.

Elenda never would have suspected Liam had it in him.

Her smile mirrored his as she turned to her right.

"My name's Elenda."

Author of Songs in the Mountain and Legacy of the Land
KARI KILGORE
IN THE PINES

To my grandfather, Fred Steffey

A long-working railroad man,
Quick with a laugh and a smile,
Even quicker with a tall tale.

Chapter 1

2015

Mary Robbins stretched her legs out, groaning at the warmth of the fire against her aching feet and muscles. The ancient oak, maple, and locust trees soaring overhead sported dark green leaves poking through the bright springtime shades, but a distinct chill lingered in the North Georgia early evening air.

The view across the granite and limestone gorge opened up barely twenty yards away, the river at the bottom hundreds of feet below as musical as it was beautiful. A skeletal frame of bright new wood suggested what the observation deck would look like in a couple of weeks. The gorgeous scenery would draw people to the grand opening, and the bike trail she was helping build would bring them back.

The antiquated narrow-gauge rails were long since removed, probably hauled off for scrap decades before, saving the crew gathered around the fire the work of pulling them up now. A stack of decaying cross ties waited beside the emerging bike trail for the four-wheelers and bigger ATVs to carry away.

Those same noisy, stinky vehicles would be banned from this

trail once it opened, but Mary and everyone else working on the trail was glad they were here for this phase.

The road and parking lot less than a mile away weren't passable yet, and no one wanted to pack in the heavy equipment, food, or camping gear miles on foot or on a bicycle. Opening day in June would be soon enough to tackle this steep climb without any fossil fuel assistance.

Mary held her hands out to the heat of the fire, her pale palms contrasting with her much darker hands and arms, then brushed her fingers over the cargo pocket on her thigh.

The strange watch she'd found was still there.

She'd noticed the glint of the gold case beside one of the tracks the ATVs had churned in the red clay right before the crew knocked off for the night. She was almost certain it was an antique railroad watch. Even in a coating of that heavy soil, it looked remarkably like one her great-uncle carried.

She wasn't sure why she'd slipped it into her pocket instead of turning it in for the museum in the ghost of a town at the bottom of the mountain. She planned to do just that. Eventually. A strange catch in her mind, and in her heart, begged her to hold onto it just a little bit longer.

As if anyone around her could read her vaguely guilty thoughts, Mary jumped when an empty water bottle bounced off her thigh. Lisa Dewey, the crew leader, grinned at Mary.

"Still with us, Ms. Robbins? We can help you get your tent set up if you're ready to crash."

"Not just yet," Mary said, unable to hide a yawn. "I'm not about to be first to bed in this bunch."

Fifteen people, half men, half women, were getting this trail through the North Georgia mountains cleaned up and ready to go. Mary had taken several of these working vacations with the three women sitting closest to her, and with her wife, but she hadn't been out on a trail for a little over two years now.

Not since Rachel died.

Long absence from such hard work had her feeling the strain, but this was also her first bike trail. With a cleared railway there wasn't much digging through roots or struggling with boulders as on a brand new forest path, but shoveling endless loads of huge ballast gravel, then increasingly smaller layers over top of it had her back, hands, and shoulders aching. Tomorrow they'd shift to building several raised platforms for camping and a restroom facility before moving to the next trail section.

"Don't worry about it, Mar," her friend Mia Chen said, pulling the clip out of her long, shining black hair. "I'll go first, as usual."

"Looks to me like the rest of us aren't far behind," Lisa said. "Bike trails are a bit tougher than most people expect. I'll let you all sleep in before we turn into carpenters. Breakfast at eight, then we're back at it."

Mary let Mia pretend to help her up, though she certainly would have overbalanced her dainty friend. Mia stood not quite as high as Mary's shoulder.

"I'm even more jealous of your new 'do after today," Mia said. "This mop on my head is burning me up, but Josh whines when I cut it."

Mary touched her dark brown hair, the barely quarter inch of curls tight and strangely thick under her fingers. She hadn't gotten used to that change yet, but it was far cooler.

"Yeah, Rachel liked mine longer, too."

"Oh hell, I'm sorry." Mia closed her eyes and turning her head away. "I'm too weary to keep track of my mouth. Need help with your setup?"

Mary knew her friend was just worried about her, but the taboo subjects and anxious glances her way were getting on her nerves. If Mia was convinced Mary wasn't ready for this, why had she badgered and pushed for the trip in the first place?

"Nah, I'm good." Mary waved toward the far end of the clearing. "I think I'm heading out to those pines over there. We drove up to Michigan to camp all the time when I was a kid. The breeze sounds amazing through them at night. I always slept like a baby."

Mia's dark brown eyes widened, but she couldn't quite hide her smile. She'd been on almost all of these trail building trips with

Mary and Rachel over the past several years. Fear didn't seem to be a part of her reality, much less her vocabulary.

"Right next to the woods? Good luck with that."

Mary didn't think twice about setting up far away from the rest of the group, not anymore. She'd started having awful nightmares when the car crash took Rachel. They were different from night to night, but it was generally variations on a theme. What Mary could have done to stop it, or at least stop it enough to still have Rachel. Who, or what, she could have bargained with to make it turn out any other way.

She knew her dreams would keep anyone sleeping near her awake all night.

The mesh skylight in her cozy tent made for fantastic star watching, though she wouldn't see much under the trees tonight. The lullaby whisper of the pines would be worth it. The clear ground and lack of undergrowth made for quick work setting up her tent.

She was crawling inside her sleeping bag with a sigh before anyone closer to the fire was finished, in bed first after all. She tucked the muddy watch under her backpack.

"'Night, sweetheart," Mary whispered, same as she had every night without Rachel. That was the only thing that let her get to sleep at all. "Love you."

Mary barely managed to turn over and pull her sleeping bag up to her ears before she was out.

Chapter 2

CHATTERING teeth woke Mary a few hours later, and at first she thought they were her own.

She was certainly cold enough for that. The temperature in the tent had to be a lot lower than the fifties she and everyone else had prepared for. The air felt frozen in her nose and lungs. She started to pull one arm out of her bag to reach for her jacket, then stopped.

Someone, or something, was in the tent, pushed hard against her chest and belly. The chattering was coming from her unknown bed guest. Mary blinked, trying to get her bearings. She couldn't imagine some kind of animal unzipping her tent door and getting inside, but no one in the camp would do that, either.

This wasn't the strangest dream she'd ever had, but it might be close. More than one therapist had told her to engage with her nightmares, try to figure out what her subconscious was telling her. No time like the present.

"Who's there?" she whispered, her own shivering making her voice tremble.

The body twitched but didn't move away. Surely any animal would take off when she spoke, unless it was some kind of sentient dream creature. Wouldn't be the first one Mary had met. She moved her arm slowly out from under her pillow, reaching for her flashlight.

"Listen, I'm not going to hurt you if you don't hurt me," she said, keeping her voice low. "Where did you come from?"

Her fingers, numb from the cold, found the metal body of her light. It felt warm to her for some reason, as if it had been outside by the fire. She usually couldn't operate electronic things in a dream, but something this simple should work. Mary pushed the button, squinting against the glaring bright light.

A girl's voice moaned, and Mary felt arms wrap around her waist. She blinked several times, but every time she kept seeing a snarl of kinky black hair and nothing else. She tried to move back to get a better look, but the girl only moved with her. As her vision cleared, she saw bare arms as dark brown as her own, rippling with gooseflesh.

"Okay. You can see I don't have a gun or a club, and I can see you're not Bigfoot trying to get me into the sack," Mary said, trying to calm herself as much as the girl. "Let me figure out what's going on here. What's your name? Why are you in my dream?"

"That wind so cold." The girl spoke in a slow, singsong accent, not moving away from Mary. "So cold."

The tent shuddered, the wires anchoring it to the ground thrumming in the frigid gust. Mary tried to make a mental note to ask Mia what the deal was with this crazy weather that intruded into a dream. Her notes didn't always survive waking up in the morning.

"But why are you out here?" Mary said. "Where did you come from?"

"Been sleeping in them pines. Got nowhere else I can go."

"Let's try again. Why are you in this dream? In this tent? I have no idea who you are."

The girl finally drew back enough for Mary to see her face. She wasn't quite as young as Mary thought, maybe twenty years old but as small as a child. Her wide eyes looked solid black in the flashlight's beam.

"Ain't been nothing warm out here for long as I can remember. Can't remember my name either. Been lookin' for my husband so long, never spoke to a living soul until you. Railroad man, name of…"

She froze, staring over Mary's shoulder, trembling harder by the second. Mary had just about decided it was worth the risk to turn and see what kind of monster her sleep-addled brain had come up with when the girl moaned again. She put her head down and wrapped her arms around Mary, squeezing tight.

"Train coming," the girl said, her voice urgent but getting lower and softer. "Longest train you ever saw. Devil driving that train, took my husband away with him. Been trying hard to take me but I hide."

Mary opened her mouth to ask what she was really hiding from when she heard a strange, ringing noise, gradually rising until it was louder than the wind. She'd heard that metallic hum many times, but she couldn't possibly be hearing it on this mountain.

The singing of the rails, the distant sound of a fast train getting closer.

"There's no train." Mary pulled her jacket over the girl's painfully thin shoulders and arms. Her eyes had adjusted well enough to see the girl only wore a dirty cotton shift, stained brown and green. "Those tracks are long gone, I promise. The last train ran decades ago."

"Where that sound come from then?" The girl's whisper was high pitched and breathy, making her sound like the terrified child she appeared to be. "And that awful cold wind?"

The tent shuddered, and Mary felt the bottom lift off the ground enough for the frigid air to pass underneath. She couldn't imagine how the anchors could hold much longer, unless they were made of steel cables in this dream world.

The eerie notes of the rails were drowned out by the screech of metal as the train got closer, then the noise rose to ear-splitting levels when the brakes engaged. The girl squeezed hard enough to take Mary's breath, and her shriek was louder than the train's.

The sharp hiss of steam right outside the tent walls brought a scream to Mary's throat at last.

Chapter 3

1985

George Evans held one of his boyhood books, pretending to read. He ran his fingertips over the rough cloth cover of *Treasure Island*, watching his grandfather stare at the television. Decades of squinting and suntans marked Adam Evans's pale face with deep lines, the thick light brown hair of his youth reduced to a delicate gray cloud around the back of his skull.

A cable channel with endless black-and-white reruns clashed with the brand new television. Even with a twenty-seven inch screen, it was the first in this house that wasn't big enough to serve as furniture.

The last early Seventies model had faded to all pastel colors and the picture rolled constantly, but the eldest Evans still complained about the modern version fairly often. He claimed to despise the plastic wood grain when he'd had a real wooden set before. The new television was rarely ever turned off, though.

George imagined thousands of people in his and even his father's generation, millions maybe. All struck by that same odd combination of never-ending reruns and parental disappointment but clueless what to do about it.

The bedroom was too hot, like always, and the smell of old man flesh was stronger than he remembered from just a few months ago. Every shelf and surface around the low hospital-style bed was jammed full of stuff. More old books, pictures, and what George could only call junk. But of course his grandfather would liven right up and pitch a conniption fit if anyone so much as moved a single thing, much less tried to thin some of it out.

Adam Evans never missed much, even as he seemed to recede into the past.

The door was open just a crack, enough so George could hear his daughter Sandy in the living room. She'd been wandering around the rest of the house for the past two days, lugging her expensive Betamax recorder on her shoulder and narrating like she was on an archaeological dig. He supposed at fifteen and growing up a Chicago girl, that was exactly how she felt.

George had vowed to himself not to say a word about how many recording tapes she went through as long as she paid for them. He hadn't even fought all that hard about her determined choice of smaller, pricier Betamax over VHS once she made his head spin with technical explanations about better recording quality.

This long vacation in Georgia was already testing his vow to keep his mouth shut about the constant recording and expense.

Sandy was naturally a whole lot more interested in her friends than her parents, probably would be for a few years to come. He'd been the same way at fifteen, just without a video camera on his shoulder constantly making recordings for an advanced audio/visual class. George's plan of getting the kid to spend time with her great-grandfather while his own parents were on vacation was working about as well as most of his big ideas had lately.

Well, he could do something about this one whether anyone else in the tiny, crowded house approved or not.

"Where you going, Grandbaby?" his grandfather said, not making any move to get out of his power lift recliner or taking his eyes from the TV screen.

"I think it's about time Sandy took a break and spent some time with us." George stretched, then picked up his and the old man's empty glasses. "Want some more water, Grandad?"

"I reckon, only if you're getting some for yourself. Don't bother that girl, now. She's like to be bored to tears by an old fart like me."

"Well, she's bored by an old fart like me, too," George said from the doorway. "Doesn't mean she can't come in here and make an effort. Maybe you can tell her a story."

Adam snorted and shook his head, and George forced himself not to do the same. He gritted his teeth instead, making sure he put on at least a neutral face before he talked to Sandy. The kid was way too damn smart to fall for fake family togetherness, no matter how hard George tried to create it out of thin air. She'd just have to make do.

Sandy didn't bother to look up when an oak floorboard creaked under George's feet. She was sprawled across the ancient velvet couch, her multi-colored canvas sneakers up on the faded flower print his grandmother had been so proud of.

George tried his best to keep his opinions of his daughter's sky-high teased reddish-brown bangs and silly side ponytail to himself. His grandmother would not have kept her mouth shut, and his mother had her say once in a while. Both women would have had a field day with Sandy's garish green and purple plaid shirt and black stirrup pants, too.

She had the video camera plugged into the wall, staring at the tiny display with exactly the same vacant expression as the man over eighty years her senior in the other room.

George forced himself to smile.

"Hey Sandy. Think it's time you came in and spent some time with your great-grandfather?"

"Hey Dad. Nah, I'm busy right now. Maybe later, okay?"

"No, not okay. You've been in here for hours. Come on, help me in the kitchen. Feet off the couch, too."

Sandy rolled her eyes and sighed, a common enough reaction that George didn't even respond anymore. She wasn't sighing at him, exactly. More at the never-ending indignation of being fifteen years old and knowing better than everyone around her. He might wish he could save her from acting that way, but he knew from his own childhood that only growing up would do that for her.

At least she stomped her feet on the floor instead of continuing to ignore him.

"Dad," she whispered, glancing toward the old man's bedroom as she stood beside him. "I don't know what to talk to him about. Greatgrand kind of scares me."

George bit his cheeks to keep from smiling. How many times did he feel that way with his own daughter and her friends?

"Well, he's probably scared of you, hon. He raised three rowdy boys, remember? Not a girl in sight till my dad was nearly grown."

She followed him into the kitchen, grabbing a Coke from the ancient, rumbly green refrigerator. George managed not to say anything about the sugar as he filled two glasses with water. His own mouth was watering for the sharp bite and sweet coolness of a Coca-Cola right now, but he didn't want to tempt his grandfather.

"Finish that in here, Sandy. Greatgrand can't have them."

"Fine." She downed half of it in one gulp. "What am I supposed to do, just sit there watching him stare at that lame old junk on TV?"

"Nope, that's what I've been doing. We talked about everything years ago, I think, same with my dad. Time for you two to get to know each other while you still can. Listen, you've been wandering around recording videos since we got here. Why don't you interview him?"

Sandy scowled, the corners of her mouth pulling in to match her eyebrows, looking so much like her mother that George's smile finally broke through. He missed his wife, stuck at a business convention back in Chicago, more than he wanted to admit. With the massive, overcrowded conference center and nowhere near enough pay phones, they usually didn't even talk until Bev got home late at night.

"Interview him? Jeez, Dad, great idea. What exactly should I interview him about? How great the Sixties really were?"

"Well, kid, that would be interviewing me, believe it or not. Ask him about the stuff around the house. Didn't you say you like some of it?"

Sandy finished her soda, crumpling up the can before dropping it into the garbage. She caught her goofy ponytail in one hand, twisting the end between her fingers.

"I guess so. Maybe. I could take pictures and put the video with it, I suppose. We're gonna learn editing in the fall."

"Now you're talking." George picked up the glasses of water and his grandfather's latest dose of pills, already sorted into white cups, off the spotless baby blue tiled countertop. His father and mother were right. The visiting nurses and housekeeper were worth every penny. "He has a lot of stories to tell. Just hasn't had anyone to tell them to in a long time. Grab those saltines, will you? He needs something with his medicine."

She sighed again, but with her back to him George couldn't tell if she rolled her eyes or not.

He decided on not. Someone had to be the optimist stuck in the house with these two for another week.

Chapter 4

The older man hadn't moved when George walked into the room, but his lined face lit up when he saw Sandy. About thirty years fell away in that instant.

"Sandy girl! Come in here to keep your old great-granddad company for a little while?"

"Hey Greatgrand," Sandy said, leaning down to hug him. "Thought you'd like someone more interesting than Dad here."

"Ain't that the truth." Adam swallowed the pills in one practiced gulp, then took a handful of the crackers Sandy held out for him. "You give us both something to smile about."

George settled back into his faded and worn recliner, a far less fancy edition than his grandfather's power chair. Both had been dragged in here from the living room a few years ago when the majority of the Adam Evans Maintenance Operation compressed into the much smaller space. That same reduction of the old man's movements explained why every available spot was crammed full of Adam's memories, much of it rescued from elsewhere in the house.

Sandy wandered around the room, running her fingers along the knick-knacks and mementos crowded onto the shelves. He'd seen her do that before in their house in Chicago and in his parents' house before she made one of those videos for her class or for herself.

She hadn't found her focus yet, but she would.

"What's this, Greatgrand?" She stepped closer to a small frame, nearly hidden among all the photos on the wall.

"Can't see from here, hon. Grab it down and reach it to me."

Sandy lifted the frame from the wall and held it carefully, waiting for him to take it. George stared at their hands, fascinated and saddened by his grandfather's wrinkled, spotted flesh compared to his daughter's smooth, pale skin.

"This here's scrip. It's how we got paid, Sandy," Adam said. The frame held several pieces of paper, faded and worn. Coins lined the edges, all different sizes with oddly shaped holes punched right through the metal. "They didn't give us money we could spend just anywhere. Had to give it right back to 'em at their own stores!"

"Did you ever get paid that way, Dad?" Sandy said, one eyebrow raised.

He was sure she was teasing him. Mostly sure.

"Not quite. I missed that era by a year or two, I guess. Where'd you get that, Granddad?"

"Oh, bunch of old boys I worked with rounded it up when I retired." He squinted at the paper, then carefully propped the frame up on the table beside his chair. "I was the only one left who remembered it, least here in Atlanta. Might be some up there in Chicago where y'all live."

Sandy tapped her bright blue fingernail on a framed document. George recognized his great-grandparents' wedding certificate and smiled. The paper was thin and yellowing, the print surprisingly plain and businesslike.

"State of Georgia, County of DeKalb," Sandy said, twisting her flat Chicago accent into a passable Southern. She even got the county right instead of mixing it up with the Illinois town, though she laid it on a bit thick with the DeCaaaab. "Adam Evenschmidt and Ms. Delia Andrews. When did you change your name, Greatgrand?

"Not 'til after the first World War started," he said. "You see right below there, my Army walking papers?"

"Honorable Discharge from the United States Army," Sandy said in her normal accent. "Yep, right there. Adam Evans, 1918."

"I wasn't real happy about that," he said, his mouth turning down. "Easiest thing for all of us at the time, though. Been Evans so long I hardly remember starting out with a different name. Feels like that life was nothing but a ghost sometimes."

"Sandy loves ghost stories, Granddad," George said. "She's always reading them or watching movies about them. I bet she's never heard about the ghost train."

Sandy's blue eyes lit up, just like her great-grandfather's had when she walked in. She settled down on the ottoman in front of him. The huge footstool was far older than she was, still covered with the same strange flat flowery velvet as the living room set.

George's chest warmed and his eyes got a little bit hot, watching his grandfather and his daughter finally connect.

"Ghost train?" she said. "Here?"

"Naah, not here in the city, not as I know of. This one's way up in the mountains, almost in North Carolina. Town called Gossdale."

He took a drink of water and leaned back, ready to get into his tale. The beverage of choice may have gotten a lot less potent since George was a little boy, but the ritual hadn't.

"Got your camera, Sandy?" he said under his breath, trying not to roll his own eyes.

She drew back and shook her head, then jumped up and darted out of the room. Just as George wondered if she'd made a break for it, she rushed back in with the camera and a tripod almost as tall as she was. Before either man could blink, she had the whole thing set up and focused.

"Don't worry about this, Greatgrand," she said, sitting back down, kicking her shoes off, and crossing her feet under her knees. "Just pretend it's not there."

"Well, since I don't know what the heck it is, I'll sure do just that."

He leaned his head back and closed his eyes. Sandy stared at George, silently asking why he'd dragged her in here if the old man was just going to fall asleep. He winked and shook his head.

All part of the ritual.

When Adam Evans opened his eyes a few seconds later, he seemed like a middle-aged man reminiscing with his drinking buddies, not a grizzled railroad retiree approaching one hundred years old.

Chapter 5

"Course I can tell you about that ghost train," Adam Evans said, nodding. "Whole thing happened right in front of my own eyes. Yeah, I started work on that train long time ago, when I was not quite the age you are right now. Had too many people to feed and not enough work to feed 'em, so that was the end of schooling for me."

He said work in an old way, almost like wo-eek. George and Sandy were watching him go back in time, his accent shifting from musical old Georgia to that poor, uneducated teenager he'd been. Neither George nor his father had ever been sure how much was playing up for his audience and how much was distant reality.

"Good men on that train, good to me and all them other boys. Least till we got a new conductor. Captain." Adam snorted and shook his head. "Insisted we call him that, never mind what we called every other conductor we ever had. Came out the Confederate Army, ran those trains during the War. Thought that old Southern way was the only way to be.

"Course how I heard it told, his rich daddy bought him that command, mainly cause all he knew how to do was make trouble for his family. Imagine they was like a lot of families back then, lost it all during the War. More men than you know traded on that faded old uniform back then. No money, no land, no skills, no other way to live.

"This was a private line, now, no rules and regulations like I had the rest of my working years, not like your daddy does now, or even like his daddy did. Owners of that line, they did what they wanted to back in them days. Seemed to think hiring that Captain for show would draw people in just so they could watch him parade up and down like a raggedy banty rooster. That was about all he was good for, but he never grasped onto that for himself."

Adam stared at the frame full of scrip beside him, his eyes soft and unfocused. Despite that, George knew his mind was more present than it had been in weeks.

"One of the good men we had, one of the best, was J.W. Gartin. Came up out of south Georgia. Had a pretty little wife, just a whisper of a girl, and he had to go six foot four. He doted on that girl, never did see someone so much in love. Not till I met my Delia. Same with your daddy and his daddy, too."

Sandy lowered her head and winked at George, surprising a grunt out of him.

His grandfather sighed long and low before he went on.

"Well, we all knew J.W. shoulda had that conductor job. Put in his time, took care of that train like no one else ever had. But folks further up the line than we was got it in their heads that we had to have that Captain. I figure they was losing money, desperate to keep going somehow. Money drives weak men to make dumb-ass decisions."

George glanced at Sandy, not sure he wanted her to hear the full range of her great-grandfather's vocabulary. She grinned back at him. She didn't have to say a word to remind him she saw and heard worse than that every single day.

George finally managed to relax and lose himself in the story, one he hadn't heard since he was younger than his daughter.

"Young as I was, I knew that particular decision was bad, probably cause trouble," Adam said in a quiet voice. "Never knew it would lead to a dead man, and his woman, and a whole bunch more besides. This here's how it all started."

Chapter 6

1901

ADAM EVENSCHMIDT STRAINED with the effort of leaning far enough forward without stepping out of the line of boys waiting to meet the new conductor. At fourteen and smaller than all the others, he was already at a disadvantage. No need to make it worse by setting himself up as a troublemaker on day one.

They all waited in the observation car, easily the fanciest part of the train. The floors were carpeted, the seats upholstered with matching burgundy fabric, and the dark wood and brass fixtures gleamed.

Adam hoped he'd be able to work his way up to the cleaning crew someday. That job was hard, sure, but it had to be easier and less filthy than shoveling coal around and feeding that boiler in the locomotive.

"Adam," a wiry black-haired boy next to him whispered. He was too big and too much older to ignore.

"Yeah, Chris."

"What we standing around here for? Waste of damn time."

"Just the new boss is all, gonna run this whole show now."

A skinny blond boy on the other side, one of the serving crew for the dining car, shook his head.

"Chris got it right. All just for show. Big captain back during the war, but his daddy bought that for him. Doesn't know how to do a damned thing but strut around with his chest stuck out."

"Hold it down, boys," a deep voice said from right behind Adam. "Don't matter how or why, this man's in charge now. Don't be actin' a fool and everything be just fine."

Adam glanced across at the blond boy, the one with all the good information, but he was still shaking his head. None of the boys dared contradict J.W., standing with his hand on Adam's shoulder now.

Everyone working on that train, from the cook to the drivers to the scruffy coal boys, knew J.W. Gartin should have had that top job. No one knew this equipment or the route far up into the mountains better. He'd put in his time and earned the promotion, fair and square.

Not a one of them dared say it, but they all knew why he hadn't gotten it, too.

The whispering and shifting around slowed to Adam's right, and he settled down himself. That had to be the boss. A man stepped into the car, and Adam tried not to frown. He was old, way older than anyone else working on this train. His splotchy pale face was wrinkled under his stiff round hat, and frizzy white hair poked out around the edges.

Adam was sure the hem of the long, gray jacket should have come close to the man's knees, but the belt with a gleaming yellow buckle raked sharply upward over a firm belly. A double row of buttons, the same bright yellow, ran from the collar down to the misplaced waist. A faded red sash crossed the man's chest, and the embroidered swoops around the wrists were discolored and missing in places.

Brand new dark blue pants and shiny black boots made the rest look even more seedy and kind of pitiful.

After a few seconds, Adam finally recognized the hat with the tiny sharp brim. This strange old man was wearing part of his

Confederate uniform to go with his railroad uniform. Adam knew from a lot of examples and one experience that he or any of the other boys would be in big, serious trouble if they randomly mixed up their uniforms that way, or if they wore anything so ratty and beat up in the passenger cars.

The owner of the railroad walked right behind the new man, the first time Adam had seen him since he started the job. Mr. Pennebaker's hair was jet black, glistening, and perfectly arranged around a razor-sharp part right down the middle. The flat, rounded hat he carried and his fine black suit were so crisp and fresh it looked like the creases would cut a plain old working boy's skin.

He held up his hand, and everyone went still and silent.

"Ladies and gentlemen, boys and girls, I'd like to introduce to you Captain Jessie Rutherford Akers. He served with honor during the war effort, and we owe him our gratitude. Do your very best to serve him with pride, just as he served us."

The man, captain in a war lost over twenty years before Adam was born, swept through the car without so much as a glance at any of the young workers. Once he and the owner passed into the next car, a general commotion broke out in their wake.

J.W. Gartin stepped into the middle of the train immediately, his huge brown hands held up at shoulder height.

"Hush now. You may feel like you got something to say right now. Truth is every one of us has a job to do. Damn lucky to have it, too. Go on, now. All of us need to get to work."

That optimism and determination didn't last long, not even coming from one of the rail line's best workers. Adam spent most of his days up in the front of the train, shoveling and loading coal, crawling inside and scrubbing the sooty boiler when it was down, doing the dirtiest jobs that kept the big train rolling.

As long as he kept the fireman, Mr. Hatcher, looking good, Adam got to mostly keep to himself. But he heard bits and pieces of everything from the network of boys all up and down the line.

Turns out Captain Akers picked up right away on who everyone else thought should have his job. J.W. never said a word or showed any kind of reaction, but everyone else saw it. The Captain took to following that good man around, watching everything he did. Before long, problems came up that didn't make any sense if you weren't paying close attention.

Adam paid very close attention.

All of a sudden, after years of taking care of that train like it was his own flesh and blood, things showed up half done or done wrong altogether wherever J.W. went. No one ever caught who did it, or who undid it. No one doubted what was going on, either.

The man himself kept quiet, nodded, and made the repairs. No matter how loud or mean the problems were pointed out.

Adam could see Jessie Rutherford Akers didn't like that, not one bit. If he thought running that train was going to work just like his paid commission in the Confederate Army did, that Captain was disappointed right quick. He wasn't getting the foolish, angry kick-back he was looking for. Even after he brought on more men from the Confederacy and they all were in on it together, he drove himself crazy trying to figure out how to goad his target into foolhardy action.

The problems got more serious, and the time and repetition added up. Finally, one day when the train was running empty, heading up the mountain to pick up a load of people, cargo, and mail, the good man had had enough. Neither Adam nor anyone else ever knew if it was the loose coupling that could have caused the whole train to crash or just the never-ending grind of trouble, but J.W. went over the edge.

Chapter 7

2015

Mary sat upright, her breath drawn to finish the scream she'd started in response to the train's hissing steam. She gasped instead, grabbing for the jacket she'd managed to draw over herself.

The air still felt like she was inside a deep freeze rather than late summer, even in the mountains. She no longer heard the train or anything else, and the girl had disappeared with the dream.

She stretched out again, glancing at her watch. Just past six in the morning. No one else would be stirring yet, not after the way they'd worked yesterday. She pulled her sleeping bag up around her shoulders, shaking her head at the frost all over the dark blue fabric. It was thick enough to flake off everywhere except right over her chest.

Where the girl had been.

"Body heat," she said under her breath. She pulled the jacket over herself for good measure. "Nothing but body heat. Mid-fifties overnight my ass."

Even after two cups of scalding hot coffee later that morning, Mary still shivered. No one else seemed to have been affected by the chill, or at least they weren't admitting it. She finally caught Mia right before they started work for the day.

"How are you not freezing right now?" Mary said, trying to keep her teeth from chattering.

"Are you kidding me? It was stifling last night. I would have killed for a ceiling fan." Mia held her hands about a foot apart. "A tiny little tent-sized ceiling fan."

Mary frowned, not sure if Mia was trying to tease her.

"I had frost on my sleeping bag this morning. You're telling me you were hot?"

Mia put the backs of her fingers against Mary's forehead, a confused smile on her face.

"You don't feel sick or anything. Sounds to me like you had one of your famous nightmares, Mar. Maybe you should sleep closer to the rest of us tonight."

Whatever chill had hold of Mary didn't let go until nine that morning. She was so relieved to be warm that she didn't mind the sweat stains on her t-shirt when she finally took the jacket off. Mia kept an eye on Mary all day long, but she didn't mention their conversation until they were getting ready to settle in for the night.

"You okay? Feeling better?"

"I'm fine, Mia," Mary said, and she almost meant it. That dream hadn't left her since she opened her eyes that morning. "Too tired when I went to bed, I guess."

"Well, I still think you should sleep closer in," Mia said. "Being right beside the woods would creep anyone out."

"Don't worry. If something comes in after me, you'll be the first to know."

Chapter 8

1901

Adam was getting a drink of water back in the dining car when J.W. went charging through like a roaring bull, not giving a damn who saw him or heard what he had in his mind. The boy's jaw dropped at the foul words boiling out of the man's mouth. Before the grandmotherly black woman who ran the kitchen could grab him, Adam ran forward after J.W.

He was sure he'd be last in line trailing behind, but everyone else was frozen in open-mouthed shock or trying to disappear. Even after Adam passed by, only a handful of the older boys fell in behind him. They all stopped at the coal car.

Even caught up in the relentless need to follow the shouting he heard over the noise of the train, Adam knew he should stop too. Crossing between the cars was hard enough when the train was sitting still. Adam held no illusions about what those massive wheels would do to him if he fell.

Instead he stepped forward, holding onto the door frame as long as he could. He took a deep breath and pushed himself across the shifting coupling, trying not to look at the huge gravels underneath.

The train was moving slowly, gaining altitude on the way up to the mountain resort, but Adam didn't try to fool himself into thinking it would be fine if he slipped off.

Even if he didn't manage to go right under the huge steel wheels, he was quite certain no one would be willing to stop to pick him up. He'd be stuck out here in the middle of nowhere, the most remote part of the line, for at least a couple of days with the temperature below freezing every night.

He leaned forward and grabbed the ladder on the back of the coal car, gripping so hard his knuckles ached. His boss, Mr. Hatcher, must be far enough back in the cars that he hadn't heard what was going on yet. He certainly would have stopped Adam and pinched his ear for him. No lowly fireman's boy should dare pull a stunt like this.

Adam swung himself up the ladder, still holding tight as he could with his sweaty palms. J.W. must have pulled himself up this same way, with much stronger adult hands and his fury to drive him. Once he crouched on top of the sooty roof of the tinder car, Adam tried again to make himself stop, climb back down, and hope no one reported what he'd done so far.

Louder shouts up in the locomotive kept him moving.

He saw J.W.'s large footprints and followed right down the middle. Adam had helped shovel half a load of coal into the tinder car before they'd headed out, same as usual. The train never carried heavy extra fuel up the mountain if they could help it. A full load of coal wouldn't have swayed nearly so much, keeping Adam's heart in his throat with every step he took.

He finally took a breath when he got to the front ladder. He knelt, grabbing the vertical rails with both hands, intending to climb down to the locomotive. The doors to the cab stood open on either side of the firebox. Gaps in the closed metal fire door glowed red with the engine under climbing stress.

Adam found he could see well enough from where he was.

That Captain, one of his guards, and the engineer were all crowded into the tiny cab with the huge raging man. Adam had barely started learning how the knobs and gauges worked in there, and he was afraid one of them would knock something dangerously out of place. The engineer huddled as far against the right wall as he could without taking his hand off the throttle.

The guard was trying to push J.W. back without much success. That Captain just stared up at the big man, a mean little smile on his face.

Adam held his breath when the black plume of smoke came his way, a habit learned from long hours working around trains. He'd never tried to ride right on top of one in motion. Keeping from breathing in the filthy air, getting it in his teeth and throat and ears, was impossible.

"Don't care what happen no more, gonna put you under the ground!" J.W. shouted.

"By all means, then," Captain Akers said, not nearly as loud but perfectly clear. "Be my guest."

The guard, still struggling to hold the huge man back, glanced at his Captain. At a nod, the guard raised his hands and stepped aside.

From his vantage point on the high roof of the tinder car, Adam could see the metal club held behind the Captain's back.

"No!"

His warning shout, too late, was drowned out by J.W.'s roar as he darted forward, faster than Adam would have thought he could move. Even quicker, nearly invisible to the boy's eyes, the club swung up and around, hitting J.W. squarely on the temple.

He looked puzzled for a few seconds as blood flowed down the side of his face. The Captain's second blow knocked him out cold.

When Captain Akers stepped aside, J.W.'s seemingly boneless body fell toward the narrow front door. There was a catwalk out there, but it was not as wide as the falling man. The guard jumped to try to catch J.W., but all he got hold of was the man's pants.

J.W.'s upper body slipped over the edge hard enough that the guard was pulled forward. The train jerked then, and Adam nearly fell over the edge of the coal car.

"Help me, goddamn it!" the guard shouted, the strain of holding a man up by his legs clear in his voice.

"Might as well let the garbage take itself overboard," Captain

Akers said, but he wedged himself into the tiny space and grabbed the guard around the chest. They both leaned back and pulled. J.W.'s body slowly reappeared inside the cab.

All but one part.

When the engineer saw what had happened, a bloody stump where the good man's head should have been, he screamed high and thin like a little girl. The train jolted again when he let go of the throttle, then pushed it over way too hard.

Adam had never been more grateful he'd missed a meal in his life.

"What the hell we gonna do now?" the guard shouted, backing up until he nearly fell out the door himself.

"This isn't the first dead man we've had to deal with, Hadley," the Captain said, carefully blotting the blood from his uniform with a white handkerchief already stained red.

"In case you ain't noticed, the damn war is over, *Captain* Akers! No one pins medals on a murderer's chest. Gonna slam us both in prison and throw away the keys!"

"And who's going to report any of this?" The Captain tossed the handkerchief out the window as if he didn't have a care in the world, then put his hand on the driver's shoulder. "This good engineer has been so generous with his time, teaching me how to run this loco-motive. You would do no such thing, would you Mr. Reynolds? Certainly not a few months before your retirement?"

"No, no, never say a word to nobody," the wiry old man said, staring straight ahead at the beam of bright light illuminating the rails ahead.

He'd always been patient and kind teaching Adam the controls, too, but the boy had a sinking feeling Reynolds was going to keep his promise to the Captain.

"I feel quite sure you'll manage to keep your mouth shut," the Captain went on. "Won't you, Hadley?"

The guard pushed the sweaty red hair out of his eyes, shaking his head.

"Whole damned train saw J.W. come charging up through here," he said. "Think every last one of 'em gonna keep your secret for you?"

"We've been through this before. All we do is clean this mess up so Engineer Reynolds here doesn't have to. Then we deal with whatever happens. Mr. Gartin should have thought before he let himself into the front of the train uninvited."

Adam watched in fascinated horror, unable to move, trying to keep his eyes away from the gory nightmare where J.W.'s head should have been. Captain Akers went through the dead man's pockets, keeping a gold watch for himself and sharing the money between the guard and the engineer. The two men dragged J.W.'s body out to the catwalk again, then tossed him over with grunts louder than the engine.

They mopped up the mess as best they could with spare bits of cloth the fireman used to open and close the firebox, but blood still streaked the floor and out the front door.

Adam realized what was about to happen a second too late. The Captain grabbed a lantern and walked toward the tinder car, no doubt to tap into the engine's water supply to finish the cleanup. Before Adam could move, Captain Akers held up the light.

Adam stared into the man's cold eyes.

"Do I need to tell you what will happen if you ever breathe a word of this, boy?"

"No." Adam forced himself to speak louder. "Nosir. I reckon I know."

"Good," the Captain said, nodding. "I won't stop with you, of course. I'll find every member of your family and send them straight to hell with you and that piece of garbage we just dumped off this fine train. Understand me?"

"Yessir. Understand you just fine."

"Good. Now fetch me down a bucket of water. Then get back there and tell everyone Mr. Gartin jumped overboard." He stopped, shook his head, and smiled. "No, no, you won't say a word. Just as well to let them all work it out for themselves. Let 'em decide he abandoned the train in the middle of an uphill run, or he never showed up for the return trip. Rumors will take care of the rest like they always do. Damn shame, him so qualified and all."

Adam did as he was told, never suspecting how many decades he had ahead of him for guilt. And regret.

Chapter 9

2015

MARY OPENED her eyes in the dark, not surprised to hear chattering teeth, to feel violent trembling. The air in her tent was again freezing. She didn't need her light to know the same girl was huddled tight against her.

"Here we are again. My name is Mary Robbins. Can you at least tell me your name? Or what's happening this time?"

"Can't remember my name before I married J.W. Been up here crying for him too long." Mary felt her take a deep breath and hold it for several seconds. She let it out with a whoosh, and spoke for the first time without that terrible fear. "Corrie Belle. Corrie Belle Gartin."

Both women jumped at whistling steam right outside the tent. If this messed up dream with Corrie Belle had set itself to repeat, Mary would meet it head on.

"I'm going to see what's happening out there." The girl clutched tight, but Mary drew back. "You can stay in here. I don't want to keep meeting like this. You must be here for a reason, so let me see what it is."

She slowly pulled the girl's painfully cold arms away and sat up.

She held a finger to her lips, then draped her coat over the shivering figure.

"I'll be right back, Corrie Belle. I'm not going further than outside the tent, okay?"

"Devil out there," the girl said, her teeth knocking together. "Killed my husband, kill you too if he get half a chance. Best if you stay put."

"You're probably right. I won't be gone long. I promise."

Mary unzipped the tent door as slowly as she could, though she doubted anyone would hear her over the chuffing, pinging, and rattling noises of the train. She peeked over the top into blinding full daylight.

A huge locomotive sat where the rails would have been a hundred years ago, or close to it. The massive steel wheels floated several inches off the ground. A crowd of well-dressed people, for the turn of the last century, strolled to and from a much smaller observation platform than the one taking shape on the same spot now.

Women wore a dizzying array of bright colored long dresses, their waists cinched tiny and their skirts puffy and full. Mary didn't spot one without a coordinating hat perched on what looked like an unnatural amount of hair. The men wore mostly dark suits, though a few sported pale brown or gray fabric. All of them carried either a porcelain tea cup or a clear cocktail glass.

Several people wearing dark blue uniforms darted through the crowd, refilling beverages or taking away the empty containers. Many of them looked like boys and girls, surely not old enough to be out of school yet.

Mary knew about the derailment that had taken that original deck out along with everyone on the train.

Please, don't be dreaming about that.

She jumped and nearly screamed when an ice-cold hand grabbed hers.

"Make it right," the girl said, still huddled inside the tent. "Make it right. Been waiting so long for someone who could."

"Make what right?" Mary said. "I don't understand what's going on."

"Ain't never found another living soul out here." Corrie Belle huddled beside Mary, tears running down her cheeks. "This place ain't safe for the living, never has been. Not a one of you should be here. Ain't safe for me neither. Don't let me down now, leave me out here forever."

A tall, angry looking man with flaming red hair gave one short blast on a brass whistle, the sliver buttons on his dark blue suit glinting in the sun. The last stragglers got back on board. Their laughter and chatter crashed through Mary's ears.

The girl's grip tightened, but her hand was even colder than before.

"Make it right, Mary. Got to make it right."

Just as the train got rolling, Mary saw movement on the back porch of the caboose. A huge blue sack came hurtling out and landed nearly on top of her tent.

The sack was screaming.

Chapter 10

1901

WHEN THE TRAIN finally pulled into the depot on top of the mountain late that night, Adam tried to hide his ragged, gnawed fingernails from everyone else. He'd been trying to decide if he should run as fast as he could as soon as the train stopped, or wait back with all the other boys and try to blend in. Maybe if that Captain never laid eyes on him again, he'd forget what the boy looked like.

Adam and several of the other youngest boys usually slept on the train when it was empty. Saved them a dime instead of sleeping in even the cheapest hotel in the resort town. Adam wasn't sure he'd be able to manage to close his eyes anywhere after what he'd seen. He finally decided the best thing would be to walk around all night and see if he could make up his mind about what to do the next day.

He tried to hide in the group of workers heading into town, thankfully walking up the right side of the train where the depot sat instead of the left where J.W. had met his end. Adam hoped to blend in with the wandering crowd of boys, folks who lived in town, and men looking for a little bit of entertainment for the night.

He was so busy keeping his head down that he almost walked

right into Captain Akers, waiting at the front of the dining car. Adam thought he would jump out of his skin before he got away, or that the man's eyes would bore a hole right through his skull. The Captain nodded and winked as the boy passed by.

Adam put one numb foot in front of the other, not wanting to draw even a second of attention to himself if he could manage it. The only way he could think of to get through the night, the next day, the next week, was to put the whole thing out of his mind and never think on it anymore.

That worked for about a minute.

Up ahead, just past the depot, a lantern swung low, and a cheerful whistle echoed off the mountainside. That had to be the inspector, coming down to make sure all was well with the train before the crew settled in for the night.

Adam froze, unable to breathe or take even one more step. People passed by him without a word, and he stood alone waiting for the inspector.

"Can't say a word, not to no one," Adam whispered. "Just keep quiet. Not a word."

The inspector didn't break stride or stop whistling as he passed by. He simply nodded and tipped his cap to Adam and kept going. Cold sweat covered the boy's body, and he forced himself to start moving. Put one wooden foot in front of the other, get away from there.

Problem was the inspector was not going along the right side of the train like all the workers just had. He was walking down the left side of the tracks. Adam didn't think they'd managed to wash the blood off the side of the locomotive.

Sometimes they hit animals. Maybe that would be close enough.

Adam had about thirty seconds to believe that.

The inspector passed by the jutting steel cattle catcher on the front, holding his lantern out to get a good look at the wheels and the sides of the boiler. He stopped whistling.

Adam begged and pleaded with his frozen body, desperate to move, terrified of what would happen next.

Before he could get far enough away, the man shrieked.

Adam finally remembered how his legs worked, and he took himself into town as fast as they'd go. Away from that inspector's high wail and everything he knew it meant. He gladly paid the dime for two nights so he could avoid the train altogether.

He never did quite work out how to stay away from the memory, even as an old, old man.

Chapter 11

ADAM WASN'T SURPRISED that a couple of the older boys were happy to make that horrible night worse for everyone who'd missed the excitement. No one seemed to know how it happened that a head was caught in that driving wheel, but those boys knew what it took to get it out.

The fireman had finally used a pickaxe.

The teenagers might have gleefully repeated their story to other employees of the rail line hoping to carry the drama back down the mountain, but it never got that far. Adam didn't know if it was the unspoken rules about keeping to themselves, or if that Captain had threatened everyone. He knew for sure he never did see the same inspector again.

The only boy younger than Adam lasted as long as the return trip back down to Gossdale before he walked away and never came back. The older ones stopped repeating the tale to anyone but themselves before a week went by, but no one who worked on the line ever recovered from that night.

The head was far too chewed up by the wheel, and later by the axe, to identify. But everyone knew J.W. was the dead man. Adam never had to open his mouth to verify or deny that fact.

Everyone also knew the same good man was the cause of problems on the train from that moment on until the end.

Every bit of trouble that Captain or his loyal men ever accused J.W. of causing started really happening. No one ever caught anyone at it, and no one ever admitted to doing it. Still, every single thing that had gone wrong with the train went wrong again, and a bunch of new things besides.

The bigger problem was J.W. had been the only man who knew how to repair all of them. Everyone else put together had a struggle just trying to keep up.

Adam sleepwalked through the days for a couple more weeks, too scared to speak up and too worried about his family starving to death to quit. He watched the train try to take itself apart all around him and did what he could to keep the engine running. He never doubted the reason for all the trouble for an instant.

J.W.'s body never was found out on the line or anywhere else. Even so, Adam was too afraid to look out the window most days, and even more at night. He was too scared he'd see eyes staring back at him, sad eyes wondering why no one ever brought him home or tried to clear his name.

The beginning of the end of the line for Adam came when J.W.'s pretty young wife showed up in that mountain resort town, looking for her husband. He was walking with the other boys, all of them quiet like they had been since that awful night. The girl caught Adam's eye right away.

She was a tiny little thing, dressed head to toe in black with a black lace veil over her face. She stood alone on the walkway beside the depot. Watching.

When the Captain appeared, she walked toward him. Adam and all the other boys huddled around the far side of the building. She barely came up to the man's chest, but she faced him tall and proud as she could. When she lifted the veil, Adam saw her features were so delicate it seemed her agonized expression would shatter her whole face.

"Captain Akers?" she said, her voice high and soft. "I need to know about a man who worked on this train, name of J.W. Gartin? He never did come home."

That Captain stared down at her, as cross as if she'd told him to eat a dog turd.

"Mr. Gartin never showed up the morning after our arrival here a couple of weeks back. Sorry to say no one has seen or heard from him since."

Mrs. Gartin shook her head, then took a step closer.

"I know you had it in for my husband. He told me all the time. That's neither here nor there. I done lost my home over this. Can't weep and moan no more. Please, sir. Please tell me."

This time Captain Akers tilted his head and smiled, but there wasn't a thing friendly about it.

"Well now, *Missus* Gartin, you may want to think on whether he had somewhere else he needed to get to. Or someone else. I have heard tales of things like that. You never can tell, can you?"

That poor girl stood there trembling, tears rolling down her soft, round cheeks, watching that Captain walk away. Watching him strut, more like. Anyone could see he thought he was walking away from trouble and no need to watch behind him.

Adam tried his best to wipe his own tears away before anyone else saw, but he wasn't the only one. This time even the older boys finally seemed to understand.

After everyone else had moved on except Adam, she drew herself up, wiped her face with a fancy black lace kerchief, and walked slow and quiet into town.

Chapter 12

ADAM WASN'T ALONE in noticing one more thing as the days
dragged on after J.W. Gartin's murder. Captain Akers must have
kept his mouth shut about what happened in the locomotive that
night, but he never did hide, trade, or sell the dead man's watch.

Soon as he finished breaking that poor widow girl's heart, that
Captain started carrying that timepiece right out in the open. He
kept it on the chain stretched across his belly like he had some kind
of right to it, and he never bothered to glance around to see who was
looking before he checked the time.

The man's own pride brought him down in the end, like such
things often do.

Everyone knew Captain Akers didn't own a railman's watch like
that. He never had enough time in the job to earn one, certainly not
a fine long-working man's model. Adam heard the tales same as
everyone else, and he'd seen the truth of where it came from with his
own eyes. Word was J.W. got that watch from his own father, a railroad man for years before.

Some of the older boys even whispered how that Captain stran-
gled J.W. with the chain so he could steal the watch for himself.
Adam hoped no one believed that one, but he never could be sure.

In that strange way rumors have of overtaking a group of people who spend many long hours together, everyone on that train came to believe that watch was the cause of all the trouble. As long as Captain Akers carried J.W.'s watch, everything was going to fall apart faster than they could fix it. And the only way to make it stop was to get rid of the timepiece.

Adam never could say how it fell to him to stand up to that Captain. He was now the youngest one on the line, and the smallest, and he certainly wasn't known for being courageous. At least not in his own mind.

Not just anyone could go walking up to the front of the locomotive, the reasoning went. On top of that, most of the boys were more than a little nervous that close to a boiler as tall as two grown men. Believing everything on the train was about to fall apart, including that tremendous boiler, didn't help matters.

In the end, Adam admitted to himself that he wanted to be the one. He was still terribly afraid of Captain Akers, but his guilt over what happened to J.W. never stopped eating at his guts. So far down inside that he could pretend it wasn't true, Adam hoped doing this one thing would help some of that burden ease.

His determination didn't help with the fear, certainly not when he was walking toward the front of the train. The air up on top of the mountain was hovering around freezing in the middle of the day by then, but sweat still ran down Adam's back. His feet again felt like two wooden blocks, and his heart pounded so hard he could hear it. But he kept going anyway, toward the Captain standing beside the driving wheel where J.W. lost his life. The man was still wearing his seedy old war uniform even on their off day.

Adam may have been fourteen years old and trembling from head to toe, but that was his first walk as a man.

Mr. Hatcher, Adam's boss, swung down off the coal tinder car, scowl at the ready before he even opened his mouth. With so many things going wrong on a cash-strapped private railroad, not one employee escaped frayed nerves and short tempers.

Adam was walking into a furious knot of men, breaking the new rules about hanging around off-duty and making himself the perfect target for everyone's frustration.

Captain Akers glanced up from his conversation with the new engineer, then turned to see Adam. He walked forward with the same cocky smile he'd had when Adam was frozen on top of that tinder car, too shocked by what he'd seen to get himself away. The boy kept walking, afraid if he paused for even one second he'd run away and never find his courage again as long as he lived.

"Captain Akers, sir," he said, surprised at how strong his voice was. He pulled a far less fine railroad watch out of his pocket, a cheap model provided by one of the older boys. "I was hoping you could tell me the time of day. Want to make sure I set this new watch to match."

For the first time since the Captain strolled through that train, medals shined bright and head held high, Adam saw fear in his eyes. No denying or mistaking it, and no way the man could hide it even if he tried. Adam noticed the gold chain was no longer draped across the uniform, and his heart seemed to stop in his chest. He couldn't tell if it was because of the man, the girl, or the watch itself, but he couldn't pretend the change wasn't real.

The Captain was afraid for his life.

He was right to be.

"I don't have a watch, young man." He looked into Adam's eyes for a second, then turned back toward the locomotive. "Not one you could set yours by."

"I'm sorry, sir." Adam gripped the borrowed watch so hard he was afraid the face would crack. "I thought sure I saw you with a fine gold railman's watch the other day."

"You were mistaken about the quality of that watch, Mr. Even-schmidt," the Captain said, his eyes lighting with anger now. "That was defective, wouldn't keep time worth a damn. Probably a fake. I threw that watch away. Understand me?"

Adam stood for a few seconds, as afraid to look away now as he had been to open his mouth. He didn't yet understand what was happening or why, but he learned right then how a silent battle between two men could turn deadly.

"I understand," he said.

The Captain nodded once, dropped his gaze, and walked away.

Adam saw the fireman move then, probably to order his rebellious charge up into the idle boiler to scrub it. Billy Skeens, the tall boy currently crammed in there as punishment for sleeping during his work shift, would be overjoyed. A cuff on the ear would be preferable to that fate on a freezing cold day.

Rather than face either one, Adam turned on his heel and headed back into town. No one followed him.

He thought that was the end of it, aside from telling the others what he'd heard.

When the train headed back down the mountain, Adam found out how wrong he was.

Chapter 13

2015

MARY'S own teeth woke her on the third night, trying to chatter out of her skull. The tent was just as freezing cold as every other time, but she had her sleeping bag to herself. If these crazy dreams had to be so damn frigid, she wished the girl would share what little body heat she had. Or at least tell her why she kept coming back.

She flipped her flashlight on and nearly screamed at the dark shape huddled by her feet. The girl didn't blink or try to cover her eyes when Mary swung the beam that way. She only sat there, bare arms around her bare legs, chin resting on her knees. She stared at the tent wall like she was seeing right through it, expecting the train any second now.

"Here we are again." Mary sat up, clutching the thick fabric under her chin. "Take my jacket. I know you're freezing."

"You think a body ever gets used to being so cold?" the girl said. "Cold way down deep in your bones?"

"I know I don't. Didn't bother me so much when I was your age."

"Never bothered me as a girl." Corrie Belle glanced at Mary for a second, then went back to watching the wall. "Even growing up way down south, didn't feel it. Not 'til I knew what being warm really like. Warm all the way inside your heart."

"You mean with J.W.," Mary said.

She sighed, remembering how shattered she'd been in the days and weeks after losing Rachel. How she'd begged and pleaded with every power she could think of, especially the ones she didn't believe in, to give her just one more second with her wife.

Corrie Belle nodded.

"I never like sleeping without him once we was married. When he stayed up on this mountain. Knew he'd come home to me just as soon as he could, though. That let my heart keep all the rest of me warm. When he never came back, my heart turned dead and cold."

Mary jumped at an airy, low whistle from the valley far below. One long, two short, one long. Miles away from where such a thing could exist, she was hearing a train coming up to a crossing.

Whoever - or whatever - drove that train was sending out a warning.

"That ever happen to you, Mary? Walking around with a dead heart still inside your body? Damn thing just won't stop beating?"

"Yeah, Corrie Belle. A couple of years ago. I lost my love in a car crash. My wife."

The girl looked at Mary again, her delicate, faint eyebrows raised.

"Your *wife*," she said, sounding more curious than upset. "You love her?"

"I loved her more than anything. I still do. I don't know how the hell my heart keeps beating, either. Or why."

Corrie Belle pursed her full lips for a second, then she nodded.

"Tell me her name? I sure would like to know it."

"Her name was Rachel."

Both women turned when the whistle sounded this time, much closer. One long, lonely cry into the darkness.

"Don't think I can do a thing in the world to help your Rachel," Corrie Belle said. "Wish I could, 'cause I hope you can help me."

"What can I possibly do, though? Much as I might want to

sometimes, I can't just hide up here in the mountains with you for the rest of my life."

Mary groaned at the harsh tone of her voice, the terrible, angry words. She didn't want to be so hateful to another person, even in a dream.

Especially not to another widow.

"You the only one who can help me," the girl said. She moved forward until she was sitting on her heels, her dark eyes blazing in the flashlight's glare. "May be another hundred years up here alone before anyone sees me. May be never."

Mary reached out, and after a few seconds Corrie Belle took her freezing hand in her colder one.

"Can't you just leave? Float away, or close your eyes and drift away? Maybe if you go somewhere else, you can be at peace."

"No, can't never be at peace." She let go of Mary's hand and shook her head. "Not while my husband's whole life and death nothing but empty space inside of me. Not one trace of him ever found. Could you rest easy if your Rachel up and vanished from the world and you never knew why?"

"I don't know why," Mary said. Her throat ached, but she was determined not to cry. "I saw where the crash happened, sure, and I saw her body. But I don't know why she left me. Why she was taken from me."

Corrie Belle only stared with those sad, burning eyes.

Mary tried not to, but she couldn't stop herself from trying to imagine it. If she hadn't gotten that heart and soul-stopping phone call in the middle of an ordinary, boring day.

If Rachel just hadn't come home that night, or the next, or the next.

Mary knew she would have spent the rest of her life, long or short, moving heaven and earth to find out what happened. Shivering through a hundred years of cold, lonely nights under these pines would only have been the beginning.

"Tell me what I can do, Corrie Belle. Tell me what I can do."

"Make it right, Mary. Make it right for me, my husband. For

you and your wife. None of us can do that ourselves any more. You got to make it *right*."

The whistle screamed from right below camp, louder and moving faster than a bullet train, driving a blast of frigid air through the middle of Mary's frozen heart.

Chapter 14

1901

THE NEXT MORNING, Adam's own name startled him out of his recent habit of walking with his head down, trying to avoid meeting that Captain's eye.

"Evenschmidt! What the hell you going up that way for?"

He turned to see Mr. Wallens, the boss of the freight section. He wasn't a whole lot taller than Adam but he was pure muscle, with a mop of unruly black hair and a thick beard to match.

"I'm the fireman's boy, sir. We got to load water for the trip."

Mr. Wallens shook his head and walked toward Adam, one burly arm held out.

"Guess they never got word to you. You're with me today, probably for a while. Time to learn why all the smart men are at the back of the train, not the front. You're better off back here, anyway. I hear the damn fool owners are thinking about letting that dumbass Captain behind the controls."

Adam opened his mouth, not sure what he had to argue about. Not the idea of changing jobs, or even a fool like Captain Akers trying to run the locomotive himself. The bright red caboose was just as much the heart of the operation as the locomotive, responsible for critical braking operations and monitoring the whole train for fire or pressure trouble. Working back here was barely a daydream for a lowly fireman's boy.

And truth be told, he'd be thrilled to be that much further away from Captain Akers.

Adam was terribly afraid this was some kind of joke pulled by one of the older boys, maybe even that constant troublemaker Billy Skeens. Just then he saw Billy, trudging along in front of the fireman.

"See you got your new duties, Adam," Mr. Hatcher said, thumping a heavy, sooty hand on Billy's shoulder. "I'll miss you up front. I'm thinking this one might turn out to be no count no matter what kind of beating he gets."

Skeens glared at Adam as they walked on, but Adam was too shocked to respond. He had no idea what had happened, and he didn't care. This was a chance he wouldn't turn down for the whole world.

A couple of hours after they got underway, the dream came crashing down around his shoulders.

Chapter 15

2015

Mary leaned against one of the waist-high stone columns that anchored the new observation deck, the scent of freshly sawn pine boards sharp in her nose. More than enough of the platform had been laid to walk on, and most of the trail crew had already enjoyed the spectacular view of the gorge. Even the safety railing was in place, and Mary had to admit to herself that the thick metal beams were more than sturdy enough for herself and even a hundred others to lean against.

She had no desire to walk out over that vast drop, though, to get closer to the massive boulders so far below. Mary's rational mind knew there was no way she'd see anything left from that crash. She was too high up, and too many years had passed for anything to be left. This trail never would have been approved with such macabre artifacts as part of the gorgeous natural landscape.

But the thought wouldn't leave her mind once it took hold.

What if the clay was extra red because so much life blood spilled there the day the huge locomotive crashed? What if the white of old fallen trees turned out to be bones baked by a hundred years of sun?

What if the gold watch wasn't the only thing buried in that

heavy red Georgia clay? If any of her odd dreams or visions or visitations were actually happening, Mary had seen Corrie Belle thrown from that train right by her tent out in the pines. Unless someone - or something - had taken the girl's remains away, Mary was afraid she remained there still.

Mary turned fast enough to make her own head hurt at a creak of new wood right behind her. Mia held up both hands, trying not to laugh.

"Oh no, I'm sorry! I didn't mean to sneak up on you."

Mary rolled her eyes and tried to smile, then turned back to the gorge.

"I'm a bit jumpy up here, Mia. No worries."

Mia stood beside Mary, leaning her elbows on the thick safety rail.

"Hell of a view. I see why they wanted the trail right here." She turned around, back against the vista, looking into Mary's eyes. "Jumpy is an understatement. What's going on, Mar?"

"Ghosts all around me," Mary whispered before she realized how it sounded. "It's not… Never mind."

She pulled out the watch and held it up by the filthy chain, letting it turn. The gold and glass not coated in stubborn clay flashed in the sunlight. Mia's eyes widened.

"That's a real beauty. Where'd you get it?"

"I found it, back there on the trail a few days ago." She dropped the watch into Mia's cupped hands.

"Looks like it's been up here since the last train ran," Mia said. "Are you going to turn it in? For that museum they were talking about?"

"Yeah, sure. I'll turn it in. That museum is exactly where it's supposed to go."

Mia handed the watch back and stared up at Mary, head tilted to one side.

"You'll turn it in, just not yet."

Mary nodded and smiled. She couldn't get anything past Mia at the best of times.

"You got me, as usual. Not yet."

"Want to tell me why? Talking about it might help."

"It won't help if you think I've finally lost it," Mary said.

"Try me. I've known you for a lot of years, and you haven't scared me off yet."

Mary turned away from the view, facing her green tent huddled alone under the pine trees instead.

"What do you know about that last train?" Mary didn't look at Mia. "The last one that ran up here?"

"Not much. I know it jumped the tracks pretty much where we're standing. After that, they never bothered running another. I think the rail line was losing money anyway."

"No one survived the crash. No one on board, anyway." Now Mary wasn't seeing her tent, the ATVs, or any of the modern world. She saw the colorful long dresses, matching hats for women, dark hats to match their suits for the men. Laughing as they enjoyed their fancy mid-train ride refreshments, while school-aged children waited on them hand and foot. "That's a lot of restless souls, you know?"

Mia glanced over at the campsite. Mary was certain her friend was more worried about her mental state than a fever after a restless night.

"Probably a few ghosts up here roaming around," Mia said. "If you believe in that kind of thing. Are those the ghosts you mean?"

"Maybe. I've been having strange dreams since I found this watch, Mia. Something I'm supposed to figure out, or change. A puzzle to solve. I think whenever that's done, I can give it to the museum and everything will be right. Right as it can be, anyway."

Mia raised her eyebrows, quick as a flash, but Mary caught it.

"You mean more of your nightmares? Like the ones you have of Rachel?"

"Kind of like those, really. Did I ever tell you what Dr. Rasden told me to do when I woke up? From one of the really bad dreams?"

Mia shook her head. Her brow was drawn down, but she looked more worried than skeptical.

"She told me to engage with them," Mary said. "To talk to whatever was tormenting me, see if I could figure out what it wanted. She said that might get me past my subconscious, past the gatekeeper, down into what I needed to face when I was awake."

"Sounds reasonable to me. Does it work?"

Mary shrugged. "Sometimes. Rachel doesn't really respond or seem to know me, but it works with other people. With the monsters."

"Sounds like the monsters are chasing you all the way up here." Mia rubbed Mary's shoulder. "Think it's because you're on one of these trips for the first time without her?"

Mary took a deep breath, trying not to disagree out of hand. A lost widow girl searching for a savior wasn't all that outrageous compared to the rest of the demons her sleeping mind had conjured. This was one of the few that made sense to her once she opened her eyes.

"Could be. I would have told you I didn't believe in ghosts a week ago, Mia. I'm a lot less sure of that now."

Mia twisted her mouth to one side.

"You know I'm not going to try to dig something out that you don't want to talk about. And you know you can talk to me about anything you want to. As long as it isn't trying to get you to do something crazy, maybe you're ready to face this particular monster. Think you'll tell me about it someday?"

Mary laughed, nearly surprised into crying. She hadn't realized how afraid she was of Mia thinking she was crazy until that second.

"If it ever makes sense enough to me to tell, I will. I promise."

Chapter 16

1901

ADAM STOOD in the high cupola in the middle of the caboose, staring out over the roof, his jaw dropping at the view of the gorge and the valley below them. His hands ached from holding onto the rail to pull himself up higher and his calf muscles were screaming in protest at standing on tiptoe, but his eyes overrode those crude demands for attention.

It was getting on toward winter, with frost common up on the mountain top. The fire in the little round wood stove bolted to the wall had been a necessity that morning. So much lower, the trees were still putting on a splendid display of red and orange and yellow against the deep blue sky, broken only by dark gray rocks and white water tumbling down out of sight. Adam finally understood why people paid good money to ride this train up and down the mountain, especially this time of year.

Mr. Wallens, Adam's new boss, called up from below.

"Hanging in up here, Adam?"

"Yessir. Everything far as I can see looks just fine."

"Keep an eye on those couplings, now, and watch for smoke from anywhere but that locomotive."

That was the first worry Adam had heard from Mr. Wallens. He was worried himself, then, knowing so many things had been going wrong with the train. This view of the descent to the observation deck was beautiful, sure, but the steep angle was unnerving. The caboose was much higher than the engine with all the cars in between twisted up in the steep S curve.

Adam suddenly didn't want to think about the weight of all those cars on rolling wheels pushing downhill. Just then the brakes sang out, and Adam's lower body felt like it was being pulled forward.

"Long as we watch for hot brakes and bearings from back here, we'll help bring her in safe," Wallens said, clapping Adam's foot.

Adam stayed where he was, doing his best to keep an eye on the train but watching the view more than he should have. He'd never noticed how sharp the right-handed curve coming in to the overlook was, and he did breathe a sigh of relief when the train stopped. Missing that one would send the whole train straight down into that beautiful gorge. By the time he finally climbed down, his hands and feet were full of pins and needles.

"Walk along with us to check the brakes and lines." Wallens stood at the rear exit door leading out onto the metal platform with two other men. "Hardest load they get is coming down that mountain and having to stop. We don't want surprises at the bottom."

That inspection and making sure all the cargo was still in the right place kept Adam busy until the passengers were climbing back on board. He was just about as tired as he'd been loading water and coal by the time he got back to the caboose. He understood now why Mr. Wallens let that little stove's fire go out. Before he could wipe the sweat off his forehead, his whole body ran freezing cold.

Captain Akers stepped inside.

"Just throw it there by the back." He stared into Adam's eyes instead of looking at the man he was talking to.

His flame-haired guard muttered to himself as he stepped past carrying a big blue canvas bag, a lot like the mail bags they normally hauled back and forth. This one landed with a heavier thud than any mail Adam had ever carried. The Captain walked around the caboose as if he'd never been back here before, stopping to riffle through the paperwork on the conductor's desk no one ever saw him use.

Adam managed not to say he probably knew more about how the whole train worked than the old man wearing bits and pieces of his Confederate uniform decades after the war ended. He thought it, though.

"Drag that out to the back porch there, Evenschmidt," Captain Akers said without looking up. "Wouldn't do for the paying passengers to see us throwing out the trash."

Adam didn't want to look weak if he wasn't able to heave the bag onto his shoulder, so he grabbed the end and started dragging. The whole thing shifted and rolled, like it was full of rocks, but he managed to get it against the back rail. He stood out there looking up at the mountainside, the frost line still clear against the pines, hoping that Captain would clear out before Mr. Wallens needed him again.

Just as the whistle blew and the train started rolling, someone spoke right behind Adam.

"Doesn't do to ask too many nosy questions nowadays." Captain Akers moved to stand beside him. "That kind of thing can get a boy into trouble. Or a girl."

The guard squatted down and grabbed one end of the bag while the Captain got the other. On a count of three, they heaved it overboard under the pine trees right at the edge of the clearing, just past the observation deck. It landed in the same weedy patch where Adam had helped dump garbage many times.

None of that garbage had screamed on the way down.

"Another distracting situation cleared up." The Captain brushed his hands together with a loud clap. "Time to get back to things that matter. Right, boy?"

Adam was finally able to turn back once the caboose followed the rest of the train away from the clearing. He tried to convince himself he hadn't seen the bag moving.

The Captain had that same little arrogant smile as the day J.W. died, same as the day he'd strutted away from the good man's grieving young wife.

"Yessir." Adam took a deep breath. "Things that matter."

Chapter 17

1901/2015

THIS DREAMTIME MARY wasn't even in her tent, or in her century as far as she could tell. She stood on a wooden platform that still smelled of fresh pine like that brand new modern observation deck, and all she heard was crickets. The moonlight in the cool air was bright enough to let her see an old-fashioned train depot with deep eaves and graceful curved roof supports, but she couldn't read the name of the town on the sign.

Mary gasped when she tried to breathe in the mixed scents of roasting meat from somewhere close by and sulfurous coal smoke from closer by. Her ribs were in some kind of vise that stretched around to her back and hips. Her waist felt tiny to her hands, and her breasts looked unreasonably large in the dim light. For a few seconds, she thought it was the cut of the long wool skirt she wore that created the illusion. The waist went on forever, covering most of her ribs, and her puffy white blouse billowed out in front and along her arms.

Another attempt at a deep breath convinced her she was wearing a corset, and a vicious one at that. Mary felt a broad hat balancing on her head before she reached up. Her hair was much longer, crudely straightened and twisted into elaborate loops and swirls nearly as wide as the hat.

Not for the first time in a dream, she wished for a camera, or at least a mirror. Even she wouldn't believe this getup when she opened her eyes back in that trailside tent.

Mary heard low voices coming from the tracks where a huge steam train sat. Her ears caught the ticking and groaning of the massive boiler cooling down, and she backed up into the shadows. Several boys came walking toward her. She wondered what they were doing out so late at night by themselves until she got a good look at them.

They might be school-aged, but they were wearing grubby railroad uniforms. They didn't walk with a teenager's springy step, either. These boys moved like middle-aged men just off a long, difficult shift.

Corrie Belle was nowhere to be found.

"Where the hell am I now?" Mary said under her breath after they passed by.

She'd never dreamed of something so far in the past or so vivid. The terrified girl might have come from a time like this, but she still showed up in Mary's modern tent. She was just about to follow the boys and try to find out when she heard more soft footfalls.

A lone boy was walking toward her, shuffling along by himself. This one was smaller than the others, and painfully thin. His clothes floated around his slight frame. He trudged with his head down, and the set of his shoulders brought tears to Mary's eyes.

She didn't care what the time or the situation was. A little boy shouldn't walk like that.

This time a distant whistle from behind her kept Mary from stepping out into the moonlight when he was right in front of her. She saw a light back that way, moving at about waist high as if a grown man swinging a lantern approached.

The boy froze. He was whispering, almost chanting to himself.

"Can't say a word, not to no one. Just keep quiet, don't say a word."

Corrie Belle's voice echoed in Mary's head, telling her to make it right, make it right. This child was terrified of something, or someone, and she knew with the certainty of a dream that he was about to let his chance pass him by.

She knew just as clearly that this whole business of the girl, the dreams, the watch, all of it turned on what she decided to do right now.

She stepped up beside the boy.

"Shhhh, I'm not going to hurt you," she said when he jumped. "What's your name?"

"Name of Adam Evenschmidt." His words were musical and lilting though his voice was weary. "Sorry, ma'am, no train again tonight."

"No, I don't think I need one. Do you need to talk to that man?"

Adam drew away with a gasp. Mary was afraid he was going to run back the way he'd come.

"Can't talk to him, no ma'am," he said, his thin voice trembling. "Can't talk to no one."

"Not even if I go with you? I'll make sure no one hurts you, Adam."

"Can't stop the devil, ma'am. That Captain the devil. All we do is stay out the way."

Mary glanced toward the whistling. The man looked like an inspector of some kind, and he was nearly upon them. The dream-time was speeding up, running away from her.

No matter how many nightmares she lived through, aware or not, she always struggled to fight down the panic.

"What if that man coming could call the police, Adam? What if he brought help? Then the devil couldn't get you."

Adam shook his head, his small mouth and eyes scrunched up.

"That Captain, he already said he won't just *get* me. Gonna kill me. Kill me, kill my sisters, then kill my mama. That devil already murdered one good man tonight. He'll kill more and be happy about it."

Mary closed her eyes for a second, trying to force her mind to remember the name. The girl had said that very same thing, her husband was a good man that the devil murdered.

Every man's name she'd ever heard crowded forward, demanding to spring from her lips and be no help whatsoever.

The swinging lamp was only a few feet away.

She tried to keep her desperate cry inside her mind.

Help me, Corrie Belle! Help me save this one child from the devil!

"We can tell him what happened to J.W.," she said, drawing in her breath as the girl's icy fingers caressed her spine. "And then I'll take you out of here, Adam. You've been here long enough. J.W.'s murder won't stay a mystery forever if you help me now. I know this was his, and I'm going to make sure everyone else knows it, too."

Mary held out the watch, shining like brand new instead of scuffed and filthy from a hundred years in the dirt. The boy's huge eyes widened even more, the irises so blue she could see them even in the faint light. He reached out, and she took his pitifully thin hand.

"Stay right here by my side?" He squeezed harder than Mary thought he could. "Don't let go, no matter what?"

"No matter what," Mary said, squeezing back. She turned to face the inspector, right beside them now.

"Excuse me, sir? This boy needs to talk to you. A man was killed on this train tonight." Mary looked down at Adam and nodded. "A man was murdered."

Chapter 18

1985

"M ind fetching me a little more water, George?"

George Evans jumped, startled to realize he was in his grandfather's crowded and overly warm bedroom. His back was stiff as a board from sitting there so long, and he caught Sandy rotating her shoulders. His daughter was also trying to wipe tears from her face without anyone seeing.

"I'll go get it, Greatgrand," she said. "If you promise you'll tell the end."

Adam Evans held out his hand, and Sandy took it.

"After carrying this mess round in my head for near eighty years, you best believe I'm gonna finish. Never have told anyone the whole story before now. Bout time I got it out into the open where I can keep an eye on thangs."

Both men watched her walk out of the room with no evidence of her usual bounce. Adam sighed, then turned to George.

"Told her way too much. Shoulda kept my fool mouth shut."

"No, I don't think so at all, Granddad. She's a smart kid. She's just thinking it all over. I am too. Sounds like you left a bunch out every time you told it all those years ago."

"Guess I should lighten up a bit for the rest."

George laughed, hoping Sandy couldn't hear him. No, his granddad had never raised a daughter, much less one so sharp and quick.

"Take it from me on this one." He leaned over to pat the old man's shoulder. "If you do that, she'll never forgive you. Sandy can spot a fake or a liar about a thousand miles away."

"That's a gift that will serve her well," Adam said, rubbing his stubbly chin and nodding. "I'll be just as true as I can, then."

Sandy walked in carrying two glasses and holding a third against her ribs. She examined the recorder for a second, then settled in at her great-grandfather's feet again.

"Okay, tell the rest, Greatgrand. And tell the truth."

Adam winked at George, took a long drink of the water, and leaned back into his tale again.

"That was my last trip on that line, same as it was for a whole lot of folks. Difference was once we made it to Gossdale, I got off, walked away, and kept walking. Never even said fare-thee-well to them other boys. I went into town, found work at a restaurant, and saved up enough to get myself to Atlanta. Got a job on a real train line, and I stayed right there till I retired fifty years later on.

"That train, the one I walked away from into my own life, she only had one more trip left in her. Never did make it back to Gossdale down at the valley end of the line. They headed out after a couple of days, made the trip up okay far as I know. Coming back down was a different story. That's the one so many folks heard of."

"The train crashed in the gorge, right?" George said.

"That's right, George. It's just like they say far as where it all happened. Anyone driving that train knew they had to be certain them brakes worked long before they got to that overlook. Like I said, that was in a big, long curve, and the engineer had to slow her way down before she got there. There's a stretch not long before that last hill goes down where they'd test the brakes, once, twice, three times to make sure they caught good.

"What I heard was they finally let Captain Akers behind the controls, with the train full as it ever was of people and goods and mail. Full load ain't no time to test a green engineer. Course no one knows for sure. No one on the train that day lived to tell me or anyone else the tale. But if that Captain didn't test the brakes going into that bad curve, he got what was coming to him. Well, he got that either way. Most of the ones working that day and none of the ones riding deserved a thing but to get off that mountain safe and sound. Not a lone one of 'em did.

"All anyone knows is that train went sailing off the edge of the gorge, right through the big platform they used to stand on and drink their tea and whiskey. Full train running full ahead jumped right over them tracks and kept going 'til something stopped it. That drop was near nine hundred feet onto solid bedrock. Not even that devil Captain could survive, least not still in his body."

He shook his head, mouth pursed.

"I never did shed a tear for him nor his buddies, the ones that ran that whole train line into the ground. Whole company folded up after that. I'm not too proud to admit I shed plenty for the boys I worked with, those passengers who never had a thing to do with any of that mess, and for that good man and his widow. None of them deserved what happened to them. All I ever could do was hope it was quick and easy for them.

"Course the reason folks tell this tale to begin with is it don't seem any of them been resting easy. I heard them same stories, ghost train going up and down the line that ain't had tracks for more than sixty years. Folks on both ends hear the whistles and moans, valley and mountain. No reason why such sounds would be there. Only that reason you don't want to believe that I see in your eyes."

Sandy opened her mouth to protest, her cheeks flaming red, but her great-grandfather smiled and held up one gnarled hand.

"Might want to look into it a touch before you decide Great-grand is talking crazy. You'll find people seem to get hurt all along through there. No good reason for that, neither. That's why them narrow gauge rails are still there in places. Everyone who went up through there after the steel seemed to come to a bad end, only hurt if they was lucky. More than should have ended up dead.

"You can say all you want about things happening just by some kind of coincidence. I heard that before, too. All I know is I wouldn't go up through there myself even if I still could. If I had my way, no one would ever go up through there again. More than enough blood's been spilled. Don't know how it could ever be cleaned up and made right. Whatever ghosts linger up there are still hungry. You best believe that if not one other thing I told you."

George watched Sandy watching her great-grandfather, sure he could see the gears turning inside her head. She'd be wondering right about now whether the old man could be trusted, if he was just pulling her leg or playing a prank.

Sandy had never taken well to those kinds of games, not even when she was a tiny child. The truth was treasured above just about everything else in her life. George knew he was damn lucky to have a teenaged daughter with that as a focus.

"Can we go to the towns?" she said, still looking at her grandfather. "At the ends of the lines?"

"I suppose you two young folks could. Not sure I'm up for the trip, ghosts or no. Sitting in a car for hours ain't the best thing in the world for my old back."

"You think it's safe, though?" she said, twisting her fingers in her ponytail again.

George raised his eyebrows before he could stop himself. He never expected his sensible daughter to believe such a fanciful tall tale, never in a million years. She wasn't putting on, either, trying to be nice and pretend. That nervous twitch with her hair and her wide eyes gave her away.

"I reckon it's safe enough in town." Adam took a long drink of his water. "If you go out there when the wind's right, you might hear that old whistle blowing. Just promise me you won't go near the rails, whatever's left of them. Hardly any narrow-gauge trains left, so those towns may have dried up and blowed away by now."

"Grandad has a couple of doctor appointments on Monday," George said when Sandy turned his way with the question all over her face. "Your mother will be here on Saturday, so maybe you two can run up there then."

"Now if you want to go up to the mountains with your family, you need to go on, George," Adam said, his wrinkled mouth drawing down. "My nurse gets me to my appointments just fine when you or your daddy ain't around, you know."

"Yeah, I know, Grandad. But I think Sandy's the natural born investigator in the family. She'll be just fine without me slowing her down."

"Well, I talked enough for one day, but I got to say one thing more." The old man looked into George's eyes for a long moment, then into Sandy's. "You want to look into this or anything else, Sandy girl, you need to do just that. Don't get into the habit of regret. Not now, not ever. Don't live your life feeling like some part of your heart is frozen, too ashamed and afraid to do what's right.

"I carried that shame of not doing any more than I did for eighty long years, but it don't take near that long to break your heart. You promise me that one thing, both of you, and I'll rest a hell of a lot easier tonight."

George didn't bother wiping his tears away, and he noticed Sandy didn't either.

"I promise, Greatgrand. I promise."

Chapter 19

2015

Mary opened the door of what looked like every other house in the tiny little town of Gossdale. Wood-frame, freshly painted, lawn perfectly kept with cheerful white and orange daffodils lining the sidewalk and huge pale yellow, deep pink, and brilliant red azalea bushes against the house. The rhododendrons higher up on the trail hadn't even budded yet.

The interior of the museum was nothing like any of the other modest brick or wood frame houses, at least she hoped so. Shelves and long glass-covered display cases filled all the rooms she could see, and almost every space was full of things somehow related to the railroad.

She clutched the watch, more precious than she ever could have imagined, as she walked around the crowded space. The walls were painted a muted cream, so all of the photos in their dark frames stood out. Mary didn't have to examine many of the images before she knew she was looking at an image of the devil, the man driving that train down into hell. She read the photo caption under her breath.

"Confederate Captain Jessie Rutherford Akers, later conductor of the ill-fated Engine 429 on its last run."

Chills raced over Mary's flesh as she looked into the murderer's eyes, the one who'd killed so many either by his own hand or by his own arrogance. He wore an odd combination of standard dark blue clothing and bits and pieces of his Civil War uniform, faded and threadbare. The medals were carefully pinned on his long jacket, and the stiff, round Captain's hat sat firmly over his gray hair. He held his head high and a little to the right, somehow managing to look sideways and down his nose at the same time.

"Well, Captain," Mary whispered, rubbing her thumb over the cool face of the watch. "I hope we can get a few of your ghosts laid to rest."

Mary jumped when a woman spoke from right beside her.

"Can I help you with something, ma'am?"

She opened her mouth to say no, then paused. The woman was wearing a dark green town logo golf shirt and a blue volunteer badge just like everyone else showing the tourists around, but Mary was sure she'd seen her somewhere before. She was tall and slender, with long reddish-brown hair and bright blue eyes. Mary guessed she was around her own age, but she didn't look it.

She still couldn't imagine why she thought she knew a strange woman in a tiny north Georgia town. Recent events had left her a lot less skeptical than she might have once been.

"Do I... I'm sorry if this sounds strange, but have I seen you somewhere?"

"That's not strange, no," the woman said, her pale cheeks flushing a little. "I get that a lot. I'm Sandy Evans, an investigative reporter with CNN down in Atlanta. I volunteer up here when I get the chance. My grandfather worked for the railroad."

Evans. An echo of Adam Evenschmidt, the little boy from her dream. Mary grunted and shook her head. She wasn't about to go down that road, not without a much better reason.

"That's it, I've seen you on the news. I'm Mary Robbins. You probably can help me." She hoped the words would come if she just started talking. "I don't know if you've heard about the new bike trail here? Anyway, I've been working out there all week, and I found something. I thought you might like to have it for the museum."

When the watch left her hands, what Mary could only explain as hot chills raced over her body before she felt a profound calm. Sandy turned the watch over, then looked up.

"Oh yeah, we know all about the trail," she said, smiling. "Helped us get a few much-needed grants to spruce this place up a bit. Any idea where this watch came from? It looks too old for our rail line here."

"Well, that's where it gets a little strange," Mary said, her own face turning red. "The story I was told is it belonged to a man who worked for another line, but a man named J.W. Gartin carried it later. He worked on the route going up the mountain. Lived here in Gossdale, too."

Sandy's jaw dropped, and she blinked slowly.

"Did you say Gartin?"

"Yeah. You've heard that name before?"

"Let's just say he was the basis for my entire career." Sandy shook her head. "Assuming you're not protecting a source, want to tell me who told you this?"

Mary took a deep breath, chewing on her lower lip. Sandy didn't seem like the sort who'd try to play games or catch her in some kind of trap. She didn't want to give everything away all at once, either. Might as well go with a different name from her nighttime adventures, the one she'd been afraid to try earlier.

"Does the name Adam Evenschmidt sound familiar?" Mary tried not to hold her breath.

Sandy drew back with a faint breath of laughter. Mary's fears of sounding like an idiot disappeared when she saw tears in the other woman's huge blue eyes.

Just like that little boy's eyes in the moonlight in her dream.

"I'd say more than familiar," Sandy said, her chin trembling. "Adam was my great-grandfather's name, and he was born Evenschmidt. He changed it during World War I like a lot of folks with German names did. Adam worked on the train going out of Gossdale, just like J.W. Gartin. The rail line you've been turning into a trail. I've never believed in coincidences, Mary. Certainly not one as big as this. Want to tell me how you knew the name he changed a hundred years ago?"

"Not really," Mary said. The laughter bubbling in her chest felt like a locomotive with way too much steam built up. "But it's only fair. I dreamed about him a couple of nights ago. Right up there on that trail."

Sandy mouthed *wow* to herself, but she was smiling.

"You found my Greatgrand's ghosts. In a hurry? I've got something you need to see."

Chapter 20

THE TWO WOMEN walked through to the back of the museum, past more photos and huge glass cases full of everything from railroad lanterns and ancient coins to what looked like rusty old camping gear. Sandy stopped beside the only closed door in the house and pulled an overloaded key ring out of her jeans pocket.

"This is the archives room," she said. "Hardly anyone knows it's here, and the ones who do are quite careful and serious, but we still lock it. Thankfully one of the donations we got a while back was an old videotape recorder, kind of a special one. It transferred Betamax to VHS."

They walked into a room full of shelves like the others, but these were filled with containers of every size imaginable. Huge, cardboard document boxes covered the carpeted floor under the bottom shelf, and everything from videocassettes to DVDs to tiny USB drives lined the shelves. A huge flat panel TV covered one wall.

Once her mind stopped spinning and caught up to the odd word the woman had used, one she hadn't heard in decades, Mary laughed out loud before she could stop herself.

"Did you say Betamax? I don't think I've heard that since the Eighties."

"Exactly." Sandy grinned. "That's when I got my start. I guessed wrong on which format would win out on the consumer side, but I recovered fast. Have a seat, this will take me a minute."

Mary sank into one of the burgundy-upholstered office chairs, thankful for the thick cushioning under her sit bones. She'd had just about enough of roughing it, at least for another year. Sandy pulled a DVD with a hand-written label from one of the top shelves and leaned over to turn on the TV and a player.

"Getting these off of Betamax was a start, but VHS degrades quickly. Soon as I could, I transferred all my old tapes to DVD. I'll eventually get around to Blu-ray or whatever the standard is by then." She sat down beside Mary and grabbed a remote from the middle of the oval wooden table, leaving nothing but a box of tissues, a digital recorder, and a plain spiral notebook in the space. "Please excuse my hideous hair and clothes. It was my first official interview."

Mary wrinkled her nose. "No worries. Don't even get me started on the sins of toxic chemicals and flammable Eighties hair."

Mary couldn't hide her sympathetic smile when a much younger version of the lovely woman beside her appeared on the screen. Her eyes and hair color were recognizable, but the towering teased bangs and bouncy side ponytail were cringe-inducing. A green and purple plaid button-up shirt with huge matching plastic earrings completed the regrettable ensemble.

"I'm apparently the reason they invented stylists," Sandy said, her face now bright red.

"You're not alone. My high school yearbooks are in a locked vault."

The teenager introduced herself as a reporter on the ground in Decatur, Georgia, with a confidence and ease Mary could see even thirty years in the past on a grainy video. Sandy promised the best ghost story the viewers would ever hear, told by her great-grandfather who lived through the whole thing.

A painfully cheesy wavy dissolve cut switched to another video showing a very old man with the same big blue eyes as Sandy. The same as that terrified little boy from her dream. Before Mary could say anything about that, he started telling his story.

It wasn't just any story, a random recollection of life in a harder, simpler time. His words were the flesh and bones to the ghosts who'd been tormenting Mary the whole time up on that mountain. All the missing parts of the girl's tales and confusing questions fell into place like a mirror breaking in reverse.

Mary's tension and worry and certainty that she was losing her mind drained away minute by minute, like pressure venting from an overheated boiler. By the time the teenaged girl came back on with her utterly charming wrap-up of her very first paranormal investigation, tears were running down Mary's cheeks.

The little boy who was too terrified to report that horrible crime brought it to life when he was an old, old man.

Sandy didn't say a word, showing one of her best skills as an adult investigator. She simply held out the box of tissues.

"It's the same story. Everything matches up. Even the parts I didn't know."

"What does it match up with, Mary?"

"I can't think of any way to tell you without sounding as crazy as I've been feeling," she said, wiping her eyes once again.

"Well, let me tell you a secret even bigger than my great-grandfather's birth name." Sandy kicked off her shoes and tucked her legs up on the chair underneath her. The professional reporter had obviously left the room. "That day, I believed every word Greatgrand said. Even when my mother brought me up here a week later, when she and my father helped me with the research and we kept coming up empty, I believed him. Some part of me always has. I have a strong hunch what you're about to tell me is what I've been searching for all these years."

Mary stared at the woman in front of her, now looking far more like that enthusiastic teenager than the serious, determined professional who didn't flinch away from horrible criminals, powerful world leaders, or renowned experts in any field.

Maybe this was what the ghost girl meant by making it right, more than helping the boy in the dream. As simple as making sure someone knew what really happened. That was what Corrie Belle wanted badly enough to huddle alone and freezing by that extinct railroad track for more than a century.

If nothing else, verifying J.W.'s side of things, bringing him back from the long lost dead, might be what it took to get Mary's own nightmares to stop.

Mary started talking, going back to the first glint of that watch in the heavy red clay, and Sandy never moved. She listened intently, and Mary was sure the notepad, recorder, or camera were there during Sandy's professional interviews just to make things easier for other people.

She had no doubt that Sandy took in and remembered every detail.

"I know exactly how it sounds." Mary drew a full breath into her lungs for what felt like the first time in days. "Honestly, I'd vowed to never mention any of this to another living soul and hope to never see another dead one to tell. I'm glad I told you, though."

Sandy closed her eyes, shaking her head for a few seconds.

"That answers more questions than I ever thought to ask. I'll tell you what I want to do, and I hope you'll be willing to help. I've had a few people bugging me for years to upload some of my old interviews, but I've never done it. Not just embarrassing, but most of them were too damn silly."

"Are you thinking of putting this online?"

"No, not quite." Sandy blotted at her eyes. She held up the watch again, letting it swing gently from the chain Mary had tried her best to clean. "I'd like to see this in a display by itself with a monitor showing my investigative debut right above it. I was able to dig up a little information about that Captain before he met his end, and a bit about the Gartins. If we include some of that to finally tell their story, that will fulfill a whole bunch of wishes all at once."

"Eighties hair and all?" Mary said, too overwhelmed with the idea to think of anything else.

"Sadly, yes to the hair. And I can't believe I'm saying this, but maybe not just in the museum. Those grants I mentioned earlier? We could probably get a hell of a lot more if I do a TV piece about the trail opening after years of rumors. Gossdale is a lovely little town, but it's about to dry up and blow away. Keeping a story like this hidden misses one of the smartest ways to bring people up here. Even if we have to put up with ghost hunters descending on us, we could really turn that around."

"I can't imagine you believe this enough to put it out there even in the museum, much less on TV."

Sandy snorted.

"If I'm going to admit I got my start as a teenaged paranormal investigator, everything will be downhill from there. It's the least we can do for these folks, especially after they answered thirty years of questions. As for believing you, I told you why I do."

"More like a hundred years of questions for one of them," Mary said. "Did you ever find a picture of her? The girl?"

Sandy grinned and got to her feet in one graceful motion.

"Great idea!"

She walked to one of the shelves without a word, leaving Mary wondering what great idea she possibly could have had without realizing it. After rustling through one of the smaller boxes, Sandy sat down with something held under the table.

"I don't need reassuring, but you hit upon the best way to settle yourself down." She put three black and white photos of young African-American women on the table. "Now, which one's your ghost? Greatgrand never knew her name. I found it later on. I'd bet she told you, though."

Mary wondered if she should make a show of trying to figure it out or just point to the one she'd recognized instantly. She'd spent too much time with that terrified face to ever have a doubt. She decided to be as direct as Sandy was and pointed to the one on the left.

"Corrie Belle Gartin."

Sandy turned the photo over. Neither woman was surprised to see the name printed on the back.

"I guess it was a pretty good idea after all," Mary said. "What can I do to help?"

Chapter 21

THE OBSERVATION DECK, the gorge, and the whole mountain range looked different to Mary's eyes a few short weeks later. Green metal plaques with white lettering pointing out mountain and waterfall names were interspersed with historic information about the river, the railroad, and the towns at either end. The trees were lush and dark green, the rhododendrons in the undergrowth covered in clusters of dark pink, purple, and white flowers.

A few curious cyclists stopped to take in the view, then stayed to watch the unexpected event of a small television crew setting up. Mary had ridden up from Gossdale with Sandy Evans and her camera and sound people. Even with trail work soreness behind her, she was happy to walk the quarter mile from the new parking lot rather than chug up the mountain on a bike.

The camera was tiny compared to the massive Betamax recorder now on display in the museum back in Gossdale. Mary knew the video quality would be far superior, though, especially with the small tubular microphone Sandy tucked under the collar of her light jacket. The breeze was much warmer than during the trail work trip, but chilly compared to Atlanta, already stifling in mid-June.

Finished with her technical preparations, Sandy joined Mary on the observation deck.

"It's gorgeous out here," she said. "Greatgrand never forgot that, no matter how upsetting most of his memories were. Ready for your big debut?"

Mary's stomach did a slow, twisting roll.

"Are you sure that's a good idea? I don't want to ruin your whole segment when I forget how to speak English."

"Well, it wouldn't be the first time," Sandy said with a crooked smile. "You'll do great. All you have to do is talk about building the trail, point out where you found the watch. You okay with talking about dreaming the names?"

"Why stop now?" Mary touched the watch, safely in the front pocket of her blue jeans instead of tough old trail work pants. "Sure this isn't going to cause you trouble?"

Sandy laughed, the light, free sound of it more reassuring than words.

"We won't get into the sensational stuff, don't worry. I'm just going to tie the trail work to getting the watch into the museum. If you're not happy with how you do for some reason, we have plenty of time for more than one take."

"Let's go before I lose my nerve."

Mary stood off to the side, watching Sandy walk slowly along the observation deck. She had no notes, but she described what was behind her perfectly. The young woman with the camera followed, making sure to keep the stunning views in frame the entire time. Sandy turned to Mary, held out her arm, and smiled.

Mary stayed calm enough through the questions, managing to speak slowly instead of keeping pace with her pounding heart. She was fine until Sandy asked about the watch, the thing that brought the two of them together.

She clutched the cold metal with a rigid grip, somehow certain she'd drop it over the edge and lose it forever.

"You're doing great," Sandy said, beaming. "Don't worry, we'll edit this bit out. Adam would be so proud of you."

Mary twisted the chain through her fingers and slowly pulled the watch out. The flash of the bright sun against the newly cleaned glass face blinded her for a few seconds, but she kept talking.

When she blinked several times and looked back toward the crowd of bikers behind the camerawoman, Mary was thankful Sandy had taken over the interview again.

Faint like the afterimage of that sun glare, she saw a much bigger crowd. Instead of everyone wearing black bike shorts and multicolored tight-fitting shirts, the men wore dark suits with high starched white collars. The women wore long bright dresses. Some of them carried small umbrellas, and most had their hair piled on top of their heads or hidden under massive, broad hats that matched the gowns.

Mary caught the drifting scent of coal smoke, heard the chuff of the steam locomotive.

When Sandy wrapped up the interview, the small crowd broke into spontaneous applause. The noise Mary heard went far beyond a handful of cyclists. Easily a hundred spectral train passengers clapped, many of them cheering.

A grinning young boy stood close to the front, his eyes as big and blue as the woman beside Mary. A huge black man in the dark blue uniform of the railroad held a tiny woman in a pale pink gown close, both of them seeing only each other.

And the most gorgeous woman, her face and form known through not enough years and countless dreams, stood right in the middle. Rachel was as beautiful as on their wedding day, though she wore her favorite trail work purple shirt and green pants instead of a flowing white gown.

She held her left hand over her heart, the ring flashing as bright as the old railman's watch.

Mary heard her beloved's whisper, somehow cutting through the noise.

"You made it right, Sweetheart. For all of us."

ABOUT KARI

Kari Kilgore's wanderlust and imagination lead her all over the world on grand adventures. Her heart and family bring her home to her native Appalachian Mountains of Virginia. From that solid base, she and her husband Jason A. Adams bring those adventures to life in fiction.

Kari writes science fiction, fantasy, horror, and contemporary fiction, and she's happiest when she surprises herself. She lives at the end of a long dirt road in the middle of the woods with Jason, various house critters, and wildlife they're better off not knowing more about.

The Confidential Adventure Club

For Kari's exclusive free After The End stories and deleted scenes, discounts, early pre-sale releases, adorable pet photos, and a whole lot more not available anywhere else, visit The Confidential Adventure Club at www.smarturl.it/c-a-club.

Hope to see you there!

www.karikilgore.com
www.spiralpublishing.net

ALSO BY KARI KILGORE

I hope you enjoyed reading *Fantastic Women: A Dark Fantasy Novella Trio* as much as I enjoyed writing it. Check out more of my fiction at www.karikilgore.com.

The Confidential Adventure Club

Want more fiction from Kari, including stories, discounts, and box sets not available anywhere else? Want to hear about locations, research, and other cool things that inspired this story and beyond? All that and adorable pet photos, too?

Join The Confidential Adventure Club and get a thank you gift of a free short story and a whole lot more at www.smarturl.it/c-a-club.

Hope to see you there!

Novels:

Until Death

The Dream Thief

Dreaming the Storm: Book One of the Storms of Future Past Series

Joining the Storm: Book Two of the Storms of Future Past Series

Fighting the Storm: Book Four of the Storms of Future Past Series

Novellas:

Songs in the Mountain

Legacy of the Land

Restricted Species

The Becalmed

In the Pines

Into the Storm: Book Three of the Storms of Future Past Series

Short Stories:

Renovations

Intentions

The Garbage Belt

The Seeds of Love

Wicked Bone

The Sound of Murder

Terminalia

Little Five: A Terminalia Story

Reflections

Collections:

Fantastic Shorts: Volume 1 - A Fantasy Short Story Collection

"Kari Kilgore is an author to watch—her lyrical voice a siren song; her insight, conjured voodoo."

—Richard Thomas, author of *Breaker* and *Tribulations*